THE ADVENTURES OF ARTHUR PENNINGTON

✕

THE KEY TO MIAMI

PHILIP HARTLEY

ISBN-13: 979-8805188337

4

CONTENTS

CHAPTER 1

Activities Week

For the last week of the academic year, our school organises an 'activities week'. This is supposed to be the anticipated event that the whole school year leads up to. As pupils progress through the year groups, the appealing nature of the activities offered increases. I kind of feel sorry for the Year 8's to be honest, as they have to stay in school and do team building activities. It's not that this is bad; it's just that the step-up (or upgrade) that the Year 9's get is so much better. I mean, it goes from doing tag-rugby in the school playground to the option of going on an overnight trip to France organised by the school languages department. This was exactly what I looked forward to once I had flicked though the activities leaflet that the Year 9's had been given back in January.

You see, we were all given a leaflet of activities to choose from during a Year 9 assembly earlier in the year. After skimming through the pages, my attention instantly gravitated towards a certain activity: a trip to France! One of the options that also tempted me was a three day paintballing military-style training camp in the woods – this was very appealing. However, the prospect of exploring a new country for the first time was an opportunity that was too good to turn down.

I'm an adventurous person by nature, and since I've been exploring different parts of England with a new formed alliance of friends, venturing into an unknown territory is something that enlivens me to the fullest (even if it's just a low-key school trip to France). My mind was pretty much set on France, but before I returned my activity form back to the teacher with my preferred choice, I asked around to see what activities other people chose, just to get a feel of who would be going. I was a bit deflated when I discovered that most of my friends were going to choose the paintballing option, yet once Vernon discussed his preferred choice with me, I actually began to see the situation in a more optimistic light. In a way, it may have been a good thing that most of my friends had originally opted to not go on the French trip, as the situation of not being amongst most of my friends would probably encourage me to increase my level of interaction with other people who were in my year group.

Not only was the prospect of going to France an exciting opportunity, the fact that it was quite affordable made it a no-brainer. This came at a cost though; as we wouldn't be staying in a hotel or hostel...we would be sleeping on the coach. This wasn't as bad as it sounded, as we'd just be sleeping through the night on the way there. It was a day trip more or less. Yes, it'd be quite exhausting, but I was sure that it'd simultaneously be rewarding.

Looking at where Boulogne was located on a map of France, it didn't surprise me that this particular French town was chosen as the destination point by the school languages department, with it being right on the edge of the country. All we had to do was to drive to the ferry port near Folkestone, and we would've basically done most of the journey (when it comes to driving). Pretty good organising from the language department at our school if you ask me!

I guess that the main (and only) downside to the trip was the reality of the long bus ride. To get around this, I usually try to use the power of sleep. It's as if you can speed up time with it. The hardest thing about this though is actually drifting off in the first place (and I mean drifting off into sleep, not drifting off the road). Also, with Vernon coming along on the trip as well, I knew that I'd still have him to talk to, as Ricky was one of my friends who had opted to participate in the paintballing military-style camp.

In order for us to make the most of our time in France, our lead teacher, Mrs Perrins, had organised for us to arrive at the school for 2 a.m. I guess she wanted us to have as much time as possible in Boulogne, to make the trip and everything like that worthwhile. After looking up some images of Boulogne on the internet, it didn't seem very appealing, although the excitement of travelling to a new country for the first time was huge. For sure, it was too good of an opportunity to turn down.

So, there I was on a Monday afternoon at school, thinking about how signing up for the French trip had all come about, with it being six months since the first activities assembly took place. The school day had finished and I had just stepped into the house. The day went as a blur if I'm honest. I was thinking quite deeply about the French trip, before then finding myself wondering what I should do after school; you see, because all of the exams had finished we hadn't really been set any proper homework.

By the time I got home it was approximately 4:30 p.m. As I had planned to leave the house at about

1 a.m., the indecision experienced as to what I was to do in the afternoon was primarily in relation to whether I should go straight to bed and get some sleep. However, because I soon came to the pretty abrupt realisation that I wouldn't be able to sleep, I decided to spend the rest of the evening on my bike, with Ricky and Vernon (they weren't actually on the same bike as me – they had their own).

They had both already planned on going out to explore this new area that Vernon himself had come across at the weekend. Wiltshire's a really cool county, and the more I explore it on my bike, the more I manage to unlock little pockets of areas that are completely new to me. Riding my bike has always been exciting to me (apart from going up steep hills). I recently invested £7 in a 'bike computer' from the local *Salltons* store (they literally sell everything at *Salltons*. It wouldn't surprise me if they are the only shop to exist one day). It's not as extravagant as it might seem; it basically lets the rider know their riding speed, average speed etc. Having bought the computer back in March, I've managed to get a lot of good use out of it, with my top speed coming in at 37 mph. However, it's quite rare that I go over 23 mph, with the prime opportunities being found when going down a suitable hill. The nature of a hill for a cyclist is quite fitting, with the effortless speed on the way down making up for the toil experienced in riding up. So, after exploring the area, I got home and yes, it was pretty late. On the ride, I didn't actually find much in the end. Although, I found an old shoe with an ancient coin from what looked like the 19th century, but apart from that...nothing much. I just enjoyed the companionship and the opportunity to go on my bike to be honest.

Initially, I decided against going straight to bed, as I hoped that if I made myself tired enough, I'd fall asleep naturally when I got onto the coach at school. As an alternative, I packed my bags and went on the MegaWay 5 for a bit. The time flew by while I was gaming, and after playing three games of football on it with Westminster Warriors, the time was 1 a.m. Time to go!

We weren't in much of a rush, and after packing my rucksack into the car, we set off into the night. This was the beginning of my French adventure! Once in the car, I was amazed at how quiet the roads were. The time it took for my dad to drive me to school was significantly less than it would have been in the daytime. It felt weird being in the car as we effortlessly drove on the deserted roads that were usually flowing with traffic. Sitting in the car gave me an opportunity to have a quick look at the itinerary and how the overall trip was actually scheduled (which

I probably should have done beforehand instead of playing on the MegaWay 5).

After noticing that we were going to be visiting the Boulogne Sea Life Exhibition Centre (widely known as the BSLEC), as well as an old fort amongst other things, it wasn't long until we pulled up at the school. My dad dropped me off near the bus bay and didn't hang around and wait with me for the coach to arrive.

The coach was late, and when I say late...I mean very late – twenty minutes to be exact. The wait felt a lot longer, and every time I heard a vehicle approach the school, I anticipated that it would be the long-awaited coach. Most of the time, it was either a lorry or a latecomer who was desperate to get to the school in time. After waiting at the school for twenty long minutes I was so relieved and excited when the coach finally rocked up, that I nearly got run over by the coach driver after losing by balance near the edge of the pavement area. I was told off very sternly by Mr Barnhill, who seemed just as tired as everyone else. It was such a weird feeling, paradoxical in fact, as I was very fatigued and sleep deprived, while I had an equal amount of excitement for the trip ahead. I felt like I was living off adrenaline. I was hoping that I wouldn't experience any aftereffects of feeling tired in the morning, but, you know, I was confident that I would catch up with sleep on the coach journey throughout the night.

Because we were already slightly behind schedule, Mrs Perrins was swift in letting us board the coach. It then came to choosing a seat. As you may already know, when it comes to choosing a seat on a school coach, it can be a lot more complicated than it may originally seem. Literally, you'd think that sitting on a seat would be simple, yet the complications that come into play in a school environment make this far from simple.

I did think about sitting right at the back, as the number of cool kids on the trip was significantly lower than I was expecting, with most of them going on the stadium tour of the James Benjamin Stadium, in London. I had briefly considered the option of going on that tour, but since I'd already been there numerous times, I gave it a pass (however I'd never been on a tour to go 'behind the scenes' and I thought that it would be a pretty cool thing to experience). I was sure that there would be plenty opportunities in the future for me to go on a tour of the James Benjamin Stadium, whereas the trip to France might be a once in a lifetime opportunity, so it was still a relatively easy choice when opting to go on the French trip to Boulogne.

So, while I contemplated the possible magnitude of sitting on the back row of the coach, Vernon convinced me to sit with him near the middle, after finding a couple of vacant seats. To me, it's crazy that a short split second decision like this can have such a huge bearing on the enjoyment of the overall trip. It turned out that I had probably made the right choice as I was close to some of my other friends. Phew. I was surprised when I saw Elise step onto the bus – I had no idea that she had chosen to go on this trip. By the looks of things she had arrived late, and after stepping onto the bus, she went to a spare seat near the back to sit with a few of her friends. After all my excitement had faded away, I gradually drifted into a deep sleep.

Some hours later I was awoken by a huge blast of a horn. It was from the ferry that I found myself on - we were on the way to France. Wow, I was so excited to be on a huge ferry. It was a new experience for me. I clambered off the bus and up the metal stairs of the boat. For a moment, I imagined what it would be like to be on a luxury cruise ship (or even a superyacht), while I was on the outside deck looking out onto the waters. However, it was quite nippy, and so having decided to go back inside the main compartment of the ferry to wander around with Vernon for ten minutes or so, we came across a sandwich bar. Feeling hungry, this felt like a suitable time to get something to eat.

Now, when it comes to buying food I usually play it safe, as one of the worst feelings for me is to spend hard-earned money on something that I don't want to eat. In this instance I didn't want to buy some exotic French food that I wouldn't even end up eating, and so I decided to play it safe and go for a basic ham and cheese sandwich. For the first time I had the opportunity to pay in a currency that was different to the pound. It was quite interesting that I was able to pay in pounds or euros. In the end, I decided that it would be best to pay in pounds, as I wanted to save my euros for when I was in France.

Not thinking that a simple, basic cheese and ham sandwich would be more than the usual £1.69 that it cost in *Salltons* (if you ask me, even this is still overpriced), I went to the cashier to pay for the sandwich. However, when I was asked to pay £4.49, my jaw dropped in shock. What a rip-off! Daylight robbery if you ask me. I personally thought that it was a disgrace to humanity that people were charging £4.49 for a cheese and ham sandwich. I felt very reluctant to go ahead with the transaction, but I actually ended up paying because I felt too shy and awkward to say no (especially as I had waited in the queue for about 5 minutes), while the trailing queue behind me of hungry people wanting to buy some grub had grown significantly. In hindsight, I probably should have just chosen something else, or left.

Not wanting to experience the same level of disappointment that I had just gone through, Vernon instead opted for a bottle of cola, and the two of us then went to sit down at a spare table. In hindsight, I probably overreacted to the cost of the ham and cheese sandwich as it was actually pretty good. It even had some French mustard in to add a little extra flavour (£4.49 was still a lot of money to pay for it though).

Shortly after, Gary and Tim came over to sit with us. They had both bought a double cheeseburger with a large portion of French fries for £2 from a different food bar, just around the corner from where I got my sandwich, as apparently, they were being sold off a lot cheaper than usual due to an issue with the sell-by-dates of most of their items. Their burgers looked absolutely delicious as well. Witnessing somebody eat one of the burgers in front of me made them look a lot more appetising than they probably were. It actually felt like I was momentarily living in the middle of a live Burger Basher commercial. About forty minutes after my ham and cheese sandwich...'experience', we arrived at the shores of France.

CHAPTER 2

A French Awakening

Dazzling shards of light from the bright morning sunshine began to sear across the waters as we approached the foreign territory. The day ahead was looming and I was excited for what was to come. Upon arriving in France, we were told that we weren't that far away from Boulogne, which was pretty cool. In fact, we only had one stop before arriving there which was at a French supermarket. It was pretty big, but not much different from an English one. After wasting so much money on that sandwich, I had to be relatively conservative with my money. I felt a bit silly when I came across the sandwich section in the supermarket, as there was a ham and cheese sandwich that looked identical to one that I had bought on the ferry, priced at €1. If I'd held on for a bit, I would've saved roughly

£3.50 (depending on the exchange rates). Lesson learnt (hopefully).

After going around the supermarket with Vernon, Gary and Tim for a short while, it was time for us all to make a move. We climbed back onto the bus for a short drive. Our first stop was at an old fort. It was quite interesting to have a look at pieces of history first-hand. Ultimately, it was frustrating to be restricted to the boundaries which come with being part of a large group. I wanted to explore the town, not just this old fort. The possibility of missing out on something exciting gave me an uncomfortable feeling, especially after coming all this way to France.

After finishing the tour of the fort, we made our way towards the Boulogne Sea Life Expedition Centre (BSLEC). On the way over, I asked Vernon if he was interested in exploring the town with me. At first he wasn't too keen, as he just wanted a relatively calm trip without any controversy after the extravagant events we had experienced as part of Operation Golden Goal. Also, he was actually quite keen to explore the BSLEC for what it was. Still, I was adamant on exploring the local area, and it really looked like I was going to have to do it alone. However, Vernon unexpectedly changed his mind last-minute. This was only after I convinced him that there were already many other sea life centres in England with similar fish to those we would see in the BSLEC, while there was only one Boulogne-sur-Mer in the world. Vernon was in. It would just be the two of us.

We had decided to momentarily cut ourselves off from our group, but how we were going to do this ended up being a challenge in itself. There was a risk that we would be caught by simply walking away, and we anticipated that if we were caught, the teacher would probably keep a closer eye on the two of us for the rest of the trip, with there also being serious repercussions attached. We could finesse it, but as it was highly probable that we only had one shot at breaking away, we knew that we needed to conjure up a method that would more than likely work (close to fool-proof in fact).

So, wanting to think of something quickly and being decisive, Vernon and I went with the classic trick of hiding in the toilets, hoping that no one would notice our absence. We went through with this, and after about 5 minutes, we slowly stepped out of the toilets, peering to see if our group had moved on to the main section of the BSLEC. They had. The coast was clear for us to walk out of the door and freely explore Boulogne-sur-Mer.

Yes, it was true that we didn't know Boulogne very well, but having downloaded a mapping app designed for tourists visiting Boulogne-sur-Mer, onto my phone, I was somewhat equipped to overstep my bounds more than usual. For sure, this gave me an extra sense of security that I would be able to find my way back to the BSLEC (I was relatively confident that we weren't going to get lost).

Just to see how long we had to free roam the area, I checked out the schedule for the day and it seemed that we had about a ninety-minute slot before we needed to be back at the BSLEC. Coming outside straight from the main entrance of the BSLEC was liberating. When the fresh French breeze in the warm July sunshine wafted towards me, it felt as if the adventure had finally begun. The feeling of standing afoot at a brand-new open city, that was inviting me in to explore, is honestly one of the most exciting feelings ever. The shackles had been removed and we were ready to explore the open world. Freedom at last.

Initially, we weren't too sure where we should go, yet after quickly discovering that we weren't that far away from the main town square, we were hoping that this would be the first 'go-to' point that would hopefully stimulate branches of interesting places for us to explore.

A short time later, we found ourselves in the middle of the town square. We dipped in and out of various shops, and after buying a few souvenirs for my family, we came across this really cool French patisserie. I don't exactly have the best track record when it comes to buying souvenirs for my family, so I was hoping that the various different French mugs and ornaments would make up for the hamper of melted chocolate that I brought back from a History trip to Belgium back at the start of Year 8. I guess I was hoping that none of the gifts broke, as I wasn't sure how fragile they were.

Anyway, the patisserie that we visited was out of this world, with the popularity and the number of visitors that it attracted being far from surprising to say the least. In France, the patisseries are apparently quite popular, and it's not hard to figure out why. I'm not sure what the par standard is for French patisseries, as the variety of different assorted treats presented was very impressive. It wasn't just the presentation of the food itself that enthused my curiosity, but the fact that there were two floors gave the overall mood of the place a pleasing aesthetic feel. Usually after entering a store and being presented with a queue would be frustrating, but in this case Vernon and I were actually pleased, as we both appreciated having some extra time to choose something from the vast choice of assorted treats.

Nevertheless, I was still finding it difficult to choose a snack. Suddenly, I found myself at the front of the queue with an employee at the checkout asking me what I wanted. Vernon had already bought a pan au chocolat, even though there was an overwhelming choice of fresh French bread in front of him. Fair play to him though – he knew what he wanted and went for it, whereas I on the other hand just stood awkwardly in front of the pastries still undecided as to what I wanted. Flashbacks of the cheese & ham sandwich situation played back in my mind. I could sense some minor frustration from the customers behind me, and so I played it safe and went for a classic croissant. Although I could have probably bought the same item at a supermarket back in England, it was still delicious. Yum.

After drifting in and out of various shops, I soon got bored and actually had a desire to return to the BSLEC. The only other interesting place that looked like it would be worth a visit was the Grand East Library. Yes, I did think about going in, but after all the school work I had been through over the course of the academic year, I wanted to give my mind a rest from anything related to school work. However, Vernon was quite keen on having a look inside, and encouraged me to go in with him. We still had time on our side, and on second thoughts I came to the conclusion that it would be cool to visit it, regardless. Most libraries have some really awesome snippets of history, and who knows, maybe the new information I absorbed could enhance my knowledge for an important time later on in my life. So, carrying our souvenirs in our rucksacks, and feeling satisfied from the delicious pastries we had thoroughly enjoyed, we entered the Grand East Library.

For some reason the word 'library' reminds me of boring memories (I don't know why, but it just does), yet after actually stepping inside the building, and seeing walls brimming with some interesting aspects of history to explore, I was very pleased that we didn't go straight back to the BSLEC. The further we went into the centre of the building, the more interesting artefacts and paintings there were to investigate. However, my excitement and enthusiasm soon waned, and not long after walking through I got bored and wanted to leave. Don't get me wrong, there were some cool things to see, but after about twenty minutes the loss of interest was actually quite dramatic and I just wanted to get back with the rest of my school. Vernon felt the same.

We stepped out and sought to get back to the BSLEC. As we had taken a 'detour' by going to the library, the directions on our mapping apps recommended that we take a different route to our original one, directing us to walk by the seafront, near the harbour. I was kind of glad about this, as we consequently had a well-placed opportunity to see a new part of Boulogne. Awesome!

CHAPTER 3

The Boat

While walking back along the seafront, something immediately caught my attention – it was this really cool boat, just sitting there on its own. It's not every day that you see a boat as big as the one in front of me, let alone in a place like Boulogne. For some reason though, this boat was particularly noticeable; something about it just didn't sit right with me.

This was the first time in my life that I'd seen a boat this big, and so I wasn't going to pass this chance of taking a few snaps of the boat for my social media profile. After taking a few photos of the boat (and even some of me posing in front of it), we thought about moving on. The last thing I wanted was for someone to come down from the boat telling us to jog on, especially as this was the sort of boat that'd probably belong to a dangerous crime organisation in a major spy movie. However, I was kind of fed up of getting anxious at things like that, and I recognised that it probably belonged to some random rich guy who was just stopping by to visit some family in France.

Vernon then passed me my phone for me to have a look at the pictures, and I must say that I was pretty pleased with how they turned out. My favourite one was probably the one of me posing in front like a boss. I then returned the favour to Vernon, taking a few photographs of him in front of the boat, before we took some of us together using the timer feature on the camera. It was hard to find something to prop the phone up against, but in the end it all worked out well.

The photoshoot had seemingly been completed, and we were about to go on our way back to the BSLEC in good time. We had plenty of minutes before we were due back, so we knew that we would be able to take things at a relaxed pace. However, about five seconds after we had begun to walk back to the BSLEC, an idea flashed in my mind like an electricity bolt running through a circuit in a science class to light up the small lightbulb component. I had an idea!

Without hesitation, I let Vernon know what I was thinking, and yes, perhaps my idea had potentially risky connotations attached to it, but I did conclude that the thrill and outcome would justify the risk (whatever that actually was). My idea was for Vernon to take some pictures of me sitting on the deck of the boat. This may sound crazy, but from where I was standing there seemed to be a clear route onto the boat. We only planned to be on there briefly, before taking the pictures and leaving. Happy days?

Yet, when I explained the plan to Vernon he didn't express the same level of enthusiasm, trying to downplay the idea of going ahead with it. From having an unnerving feeling towards the presence of the boat, and with us being ignorant of the French laws related to my idea (plus the potential punishment in France for going on someone's yacht without permission), he said that we should just move on and not get involved in a situation that could easily land us in some hot water. From his point of view, it was better for us to go back to the BSLEC.

I don't know how, but I actually managed to convince Vernon to go along with my idea, emphasising that I would just stand near the exit and leave the boat as soon as I heard a noise or something like that. Although after telling me he wasn't fully committed to my idea, he agreed to do it with me, as long he didn't have to go on the boat as well, after I mentioned to him how cool the pictures would be.

With it looking like there wasn't anyone guarding the boat, it seemed too easy to get on board, like being offered a 95% discount on a brand new sports car for no apparent reason – I had a weird sense that there was a catch, or a trap set out. After each step that I took up the stairs, it felt as if something or someone was going to jump at me out of nowhere. But no, I was still going and the coast was clear. At one point I half-expected a trap door to open up below my feet. However, the path onto the boat was smooth. For sure the boat felt significantly more eerie after we were finally aboard.

While I was on the edge of the platform, Vernon quickly took a picture of me. I wanted this picture to be my most liked, and so after being disappointed with the background in the photo that Vernon had just taken, I decided to find a place on the boat that was a bit more 'extravagant'. For me, it was similar to something that Roger Jenkins said when referring to his decision to take a match-winning penalty for Westminster, even though he had missed the previous three that he had taken prior to that, during a rough patch in his career: "Go big or go home," and I was not willing to go home without trying.

I tried to convince Vernon to come on board with me, and help me look for a better area for a cool picture, but he then said something about trespassing and that it wasn't a good idea. He may have a point, as I didn't really know French Law, but what I did know was that I desperately wanted to have a picture taken on one of the comfy outside sofas on the yacht.

After swiftly convincing Vernon to come on board with me, we wandered into a room that led out onto the deck, and found a really cool sofa that was perfect for a mini amateur photoshoot. I hoped to make sure that anyone who looked at our photo would be able to instantly tell that we were on a yacht. Vernon fired away, taking some splendid photos, and seeing how well they came out (while also finding it to be quite amusing), he was keen to have me take one of him as well. I didn't hesitate in returning the favour and took a few cool snaps of him posing nonchalantly. Immediately looking back at the photos, it was hard not to laugh, with it looking like Vernon owned the yacht based on his pose. The photos had been taken, and it would probably have been best if we quietly left the boat, but as it seemed empty, and no one had come to order us off the yacht, we roamed around further to explore other parts of this interesting vessel.

We did think about going back at first, but as the boat was conspicuously quiet, we presumed that we had a suitable opportunity to explore further. It was the first time that I had actually been on a yacht, and although I had seen what they looked like in some of the movies that I had watched, actually being on one in real life was surreal. We then wandered inside of what looked like the central area of the boat, where we came across a really cool lounge area. The doors were wide open, and although it looked like people had recently been there, I was keen to have a look around.

Rather quickly, I sensed a bit of unease in the overall atmosphere of the room, but in the corner of my eye, something familiar caught my attention. It was a painting. This wasn't just any painting: it was one that I recognised from when Butch showed me a picture of a historic painting that had been stolen from an art gallery in America, shortly after the success of Operation Golden Goal. According to Butch, this painting was significant due to the apparent clues embedded into it. Painted by Enrico Gonzalez in 1921 and being one of the most famous paintings in the world, it kind of felt weird seeing it on the wall. As this looked like a painting that had recently been stolen, I convinced myself that this was just a replica of the original, as I thought it was too farfetched to potentially be on a boat 'belonging' (that is if they didn't steal the boat) to a criminal mastermind group.

I was sure that it was most likely a replica, with it being well known in French folklore and being aesthetically pleasing. Knowing that it'd probably be a good idea to take a few pictures for Butch to have a look at, I carefully crept up to the painting and took some clear shots of it under suitable lighting while Vernon was on the lookout. I'm far from a painting verification specialist, but from looking up close, it looked quite old, and...it didn't look fake.

I was about to leave, as we had been on the boat for long enough, but Vernon then suggested that I check the back of the painting to see if there was anything on that side that might lead us to a clearer conclusion regarding the painting's legitimacy. Yes, this seemed like a good idea, but it wouldn't exactly be easy, from judging the bulkiness of the frame. Confronting the painting, and scanning every corner of it to look for any potential difficulties or hazards that I could encounter from moving it, I just knew that taking it off the wall would be a tough challenge. Also, we'd have to disconnect the painting from the frame, carefully and efficiently.

This could help us solve a big mystery, and this would probably be our only chance to do this. One of the things I've learnt so far during my time in Year 9 is to take chances when they come, as you never know when the last opportunity for something is. I learnt this from missing the opportunity to buy a rare trading card off someone at school for £5 when I was in Year 4. The same card has since gone up in value to an estimated price of £5,000 (and still rising). I did want to buy it, but I kept putting it off and in the end, I payed a heavy price for it. At the time these trading cards weren't very popular at school, but they've now become a new craze. Loads of people I know have started to collect them again.

As we didn't have a painting authentication kit to check whether the painting was in fact real, we needed to come up with a different idea. You see, taking away even a snippet of the painting to use as a testing sample would technically be stealing and so shortly after searching my mind for ideas, I had the idea of taking the picture off the wall, to get some more angles of the painting, as well as getting a clear look at the back of it. Considering the options, this definitely seemed to be the best alternative, especially considering that we were in a rush to get off the boat ASAP.

So, I carefully took the painting off the wall. From all the tension that had ensued, my fingers began to feel slightly sweaty, and while taking it off, thoughts of the painting slipping through my fingers rang around in my mind like...well I'm not sure what it was like exactly, as it was quite a unique experience – there isn't really something that I could compare it to. Fortunately, I did manage to get the painting off and onto the table – demonstrating that giving into the anxiety wouldn't have been useful. However, once I had placed the painting on the table, I ran into another problem: we needed to find a way to detach the painting from the frame. I thought I might have to resort to vandalising the frame in order to gain access to the painting in the short time span that we had, but our job was nowhere near this hard, as the frame had a small button to detach itself from the painting; it felt too easy.

After 'unlocking' the mechanism that was holding the frame together through the click of a button, Vernon assisted me in carefully opening the back latch up. We needed to have a suitable angle for a clear photograph as well as taking the lighting into consideration. We didn't take the painting out of the room or anything like that, but we did move it to a nearby pool table, as putting it there gave us some really good lighting. Placing the painting on the table, a faint outline of a map suddenly emerged before our very eyes. I can't put my thumb on it, but for sure there was something special about this painting that made it different to others that I had seen in person before. I was sure that this was the real deal. I had no idea of the location that the map was of, but nonetheless we took some helpful photographs for us to look at later. After taking a burst of small pictures, we heard footsteps in the not-so-distant background. We needed to leave.

I knew that I needed to hide, and so without any further consideration of what to do, I rapidly took a further splurge of photographs of the back of the painting, before scanning the room for a hiding place. I desperately wanted to put it back on the wall, but being limited on time, hiding was suddenly the priority. Usually when I'm looking for a place to hide, I at least get a thirty second countdown during a game of hide-and-seek, but here I found myself in significantly different circumstance. We literally had a matter of seconds. We looked around and had no idea where to go. In the corner of my eye I then saw two dudes approaching the lounging area. The situation was dire, and I momentarily froze like a rabbit in headlights.

However, at the last second, I noticed the main dining room table, and instinctively dived underneath it like a rugby player diving towards the try line in a cup final. Although, the table was relatively exposed, the table cloth gave me some adequate cover, while I was also sure that this was better than aimlessly standing out in the open, waiting to be apprehended.

The fact that the painting was off the wall didn't look too good, and I further hoped that the two guys who came in didn't resort to having dinner. All I could do was to stay as silent as possible and hope that I didn't get noticed. Even though the situation was very tense, I couldn't help but get a view of what they were doing. And as for Vernon, well, I had no idea where he had gone to. For all I know he could have left the boat and gone on towards the BSLEC. I thought about messaging him to see where he had got to, but I didn't want to turn my phone on in case my phone went off - it was too risky.

Then, two men entered. Apart from a few whispers and murmurs, neither said a word to each other and were in fact very quiet. Going over to where the painting would have been hung up, the tension in the room was cranked up a notch when they noticed it wasn't there. It was obvious that this is what they were on the boat for. I was in suspense as the chance of them looking for the painting under the dining table seemed palpably high. However, after they imminently noticed it on the pool table opposite, my anxiety was instantly quelled. It was very hard to gain an understanding from any clues of who they were, as they weren't around for very long. After standing around the painting for about a minute, they left and that was that. Still, I needed to leave ASAP, and just to make sure the coast was clear and that they had actually gone, I waited further for a short while (probably 5 minutes, although I wasn't sure as I didn't have any way of checking the time) before looking to leave my point of refuge, underneath the luxurious dining table.

After it had felt like long enough, and having a solid sense of assurance, I sprang up out from underneath the table and began to dart off the boat as fast I could. I was hoping that if I was spotted that I would be able to outrun the possibility of someone chasing after me. Yes, I'm not the fastest, but I certainly had a head start if this did occur.

Just I was about to leave the boat, a frantic realisation surfaced — I suddenly remembered about Vernon! I had no idea where he had got to since I hid from the two mysterious men who came in. Because I assumed that the two guys were no longer on the boat (mainly because I saw them both step off it — well, I think I did anyway), I thought that it would be relatively safe to look for Vernon. Although the boat was big, I thought that if I quietly had a look around for him, I could at least leave the boat knowing that I had tried my best (considering the circumstances) to look for Vernon.

CHAPTER 4

Escape

I checked my messages, and there was nothing from Vernon. I did have one from Elise though, asking where I was, as she said that the people were meeting up in their groups ready to end the visit. Wanting to not waste any more precious seconds looking for Vernon, and also needing to be attentive for anyone else who may be on board, I replied to Elise with a running emoji – I didn't exactly want her and the whole school finding out that I was on a potentially shady yacht, looking for one of my other class mates.

After stealthily coasting through around the yacht, I came across some stairs leading to the top deck. Step by step I went up, and I was about to go onto the top deck, when I suddenly noticed a group of people on there. From looking at their apparel, they were all dressed differently to the guys who I saw earlier. I can only go by trousers and footwear, yet something about the two guys from earlier still didn't sit right with me. It also made me curious as to why there wasn't any security when Vernon and I first came on board the boat. It's as if the group of 4 on the top deck were oblivious to the happenings on the deck below. You'd think that there would be some sort of substantial security on a boat as big and flashy as the one I found myself on! It was also strange that they were here in Boulogne. I mean no disrespect to this place, but it's not exactly the most exotic or luxurious location to visit.

With people on the top deck, it seemed obvious that Vernon wouldn't be up there if he was still actually on the boat, and so I decided to quickly skim through the bedrooms, just in case Vernon was under one of the beds or something. The longer I was on the boat, the more I just wanted to get off it. The idea of getting on board just to take a picture seemed so unimportant and distant at this moment in time, and what made it worse was that the rest of my school at the BSLEC were probably wondering where I was. With an increase in the circumstantial intensity, each precious second dramatically ticked by.

Before going down the stairs, I checked a nearby room, as from the size and locality of it (and because I know Vernon quite well) it had qualities for a good hiding place. Slowly and carefully, I gently eased myself through the doorway, into the room. As the lights weren't on, it would seem obvious to the average passer-by that the room was vacant. Yet, I was still wary of someone jumping at me, and using the light seeping in from the outside corridor area, I was able to make out the basic features of the room. I did think about turning the light on, but I wanted to be almost certain that a user of the boat wasn't in the room sleeping. Frighteningly, this was exactly what I thought I saw.

From the light gently flowing through from the surrounding doorway, I made out what looked like a hand. I was sure that this would be the last place that someone on the yacht would want to sleep, so I thought that if it was someone, it would be Vernon, who may have found somewhere to hide before then drifting off to sleep. Deciding that this was the best time to finally switch on the light, I felt around on the wall for the light switch but I couldn't find it. However, I was okay for light, and reassuringly switched on my phone light instead.

As soon as my light illuminated the room, I experienced a feeling I had never experienced before. The person lying on the floor wasn't Vernon, but he had what looked like a black eye and a busted-up nose that had blood running from it. He looked unconscious. Judging from what the guy was wearing, it didn't take me long to figure out the likelihood of him working as a security guard on the boat. His unfortunate predicament probably explained how Vernon and I were able to get on the boat so easily. Judging from the supposed security guard's poundings, it looked as if he hadn't been long since he had presumably been beaten up, which consequently led me to believe that the two guys who I was hiding from earlier had probably done the damage as imposters. The question was, why would they do this, and what did they want with the painting?

So, fortunately there was a first aid box nearby, and after putting the guy in a recovery position and attending to his wounds, I made my way downstairs in a stealth-like manner to have a quick look for Vernon. If I wasn't able to find him, it would be up to him to find his way back to the BSLEC (after I had texted him of course). The security guard woke up though and started to walk after me. I still needed to find Vernon, or at least have a check to see whether or not he was on the boat. The guard wasn't able to run at 100%, but he was still able to put up a good chase.

Still feeling uneasy chills from the surroundings, I came across the master cabin with one of the biggest beds I'd ever seen. I quickly looked underneath, and there and behold was Vernon – I was glad I didn't leave him, while he was equally glad to see me, but I didn't have time for any introductory formalities. I had to tell him about the situation and that we needed to get off the boat as quickly as possible. Vaguely having an idea of the boat's layout, we ran up the stairs onto the tier with the lounge on, ready to make our way off, and then make our way back to the BSLEC.

As we made our way through the lounge I suddenly became startled at what I saw – the painting had gone! I did not want to get involved in what was a potential high-level criminal investigation (I had already gone as far into that world as I would have liked during the English Cup Final, and it was not something that I was keen on going through again).

With the painting gone, I was half-hoping that the security guard hadn't alerted an entourage of people to come after us, especially if they saw that the painting had disappeared, and thought we had taken it. Suddenly the security guard saw that the painting was missing, and then sprang forward towards us as if he hadn't been knocked out, and lunged at us. I wasn't really worried about what he could do to me as he was limping after his first few steps – I was more concerned about what the other people on the boat might do to me if they caught hold of me! With the guard then alerting everyone on the boat and shouting after us, we accelerated our efforts to jump off the boat (onto the platform of course, and within appropriate jumping distance).

I thought that we would be fine once we were off the boat, with an easy walk back to the BSLEC. Yet after peering over my shoulder and seeing that the two guys who had been sitting up top were after us, a sense of desperation gushed into my psyche. Splitting up was not an option, with the town completely new to us, we knew that having each other's back would help us form a desperate getaway. I had so much adrenaline rushing through my body that I felt like I could run a 100m sprint in 9.57 seconds. Without much knowledge of where I was going, I took lead with Vernon just behind me. We legged it for the town centre.

We weren't sure whether to try and outrun them, or hide away in one of the buildings. After peering over my shoulder and seeing that both of the guys were still hot on our heels (and gaining), I anticipated that our best chance of success would be to slip into one of the nearby buildings. Yet, this was also risky, as I didn't know the area at all, and the thought of running into a dead-end made me shudder, motivating me to keep on running. With the two men gaining on us as each second passed by, memories of the time when I had to outrun Connor back at school flooded back to the forefront of my mind. It's crazy how recent that incident actually was, with so many significant events in my life having taken place since.

To my right, Vernon looked as if he was about to give up, and I was thinking of doing the same. My hope of outrunning these guys was wearing thin, with people stopping and gazing at what looked like an Olympic race happening before their eyes. We ran around a corner, and just as I was about to stop and give myself up to these potentially dangerous people, I saw the town library ahead of me (the same one that we had previously had a look around). As this was one of the biggest buildings in the town (and I even had a rough idea of the layout of the place), a spark of hope invigorated my being, fuelling my motivation to carry on just a little bit further into this building. It was probably 150 ft. ahead at the end of the street.

I quickly communicated this plan to Vernon, and with him leading the charge, we raced through the street and towards the library doors as fast as something that goes as fast as we were going could (which was pretty fast, I'm just not sure how fast specifically). Fortunately, we had enough speed to evade the guys who were chasing us.

Missing a librarian carrying a few books back to some bookshelves by a matter of inches, we raced through the library desperately looking for a place to camp out and leave. Once we were inside though, we had no idea what to do. Vernon suggested that we hide by the main entrance, and then quietly sneak out once the two guys had hopefully gone past us. This was an interesting idea, and would have been an easy one to follow, yet the main problem was that there wasn't anywhere to hide. Hiding behind the main desk might have worked, but after nearly knocking the main librarian over, I didn't think she would be too enthusiastic about helping us in this situation. On the whole, there wasn't really an obvious place to hide inside. The best idea we were able to conjure up, was to hide between the rows of shelves and continuously move about. Curiously, I leant and pressed against an ancient looking bookshelf in the corner of the library, just in case it led to a secret chamber of some sort. It didn't.

After scrambling around, we found an appropriate row and stood there, waiting, and trying to act as natural as possible - we also had a good view of the main entrance, which was an added bonus. Abruptly, we saw the duo enter through the main entrance and head straight to the toilets.

Either they were really desperate for the loo, or they thought that we were hiding in there. Whichever, this was our chance to leave unnoticed. Vernon agreed with this, and we both rushed towards the door trying to make a swift exit. The only downside to all of this would be if they came out at the same time we went through the door. Fortunately they didn't and in an attempt to keep and maintain a low profile, we calmly walked away.

After looking at the map app on our phones, it said that the BSLEC was only a ten minute walk away from the where we were. With this being our next stop, I hoped that the school hadn't worried where we were, although from the looks of the messages that I was getting from Elise, there seemed to be some commotion as to where Vernon and I had got to.

CHAPTER 5

Solace in BSLEC

After tentatively and cautiously making our way
through the streets of Boulogne to the BSLEC, we had
to think of a way to re-join the rest of the group
without causing any drama. We had to do this
smoothly, with a touch of finesse. Through messaging
Elise for some information on how the situation inside
was, I discovered that the teachers were beginning to
get quite anxious, with employees searching for us
around the venue. I guess that this is understandable,
as it would be difficult for a teacher to tell a parent
about their child disappearing in a foreign country.
The longer the search went on, the harder it would be
to reveal ourselves, so we decided to just take the hit
and come back in as soon as possible.

We went over to reception, and instantly the
class recognised us approaching, letting the teachers
know of our presence. The reaction from Mrs Perrins
was a mixed one to say the least, as she seemed
relieved that we weren't lost, while simultaneously
being furious at us for disappearing.

While I was happy to have made it to the BSLEC unscathed, the fact that moments ago Vernon and I had two full-grown dudes chasing after us still made me feel uneasy. With this thought hanging around in the back of my mind, I was still wondering where they were, I mean, did they actually know where we were, with a plan to find us later? With these thoughts whirling, I desired to sit down quietly somewhere and relax inside for a short while.

I felt a bit downbeat about how the trip had gone, yet I soon picked myself up again and simply chose to make the most of it – I still had the photographs of the painting and the whole situation could have been a lot worse. I managed to briefly talk with Elise, who appeared slightly concerned as to what I had actually been doing, as from my messages she said that it looked as if I may have found myself in a sticky situation. I wasn't sure whether to tell her what happened or let it slide. In the end I didn't think it was worth explaining it to her, as I just wanted to take my mind off everything that had happened, sit back, relax, and enjoy the rest of the trip.

Making our way outside, the teachers gave us all a bit of free time to explore the local area (which I had kind of already done, but this time, I definitely wanted to stay out of trouble). I don't know if it had anything to do with us, or if it's just the way things are in France, but there were a lot of police officers on the streets roaming around different shops. It did make me wonder whether it had anything to do with the painting, as I hoped that, if it did get stolen without being recovered, people wouldn't think it was us. Just to be on the safe side, I bought some new clothes, with sunglasses and a hat from a cheap discount store that we came across – you just never know who you could run into. Thinking that this was a good idea, Vernon also did the same, yet he opted out when it came to buying sunglasses. It was useful having Elise with us as well, as this would make it harder to think that the two kids running through the straights an hour or so ago was us, as we were now wearing completely different clothes, while we were also no longer roaming the streets as a pair.

After the three of us had visited a few interesting shops to get some souvenirs, Elise suggested that we get something to eat with the remaining time that we had left. At first, I was a bit on edge about bumping into one of the guys who had previously chased after Vernon and I. However, once we did get into the restaurant, after having a brief look around, the coast seemed clear.

The restaurant that we found was kind of fancy, and with the sunshine out blazing, and because of the calm wafting breeze that had dominated the outside climate, getting a seat on the balcony overlooking the harbour was a huge priority. While walking over to the balcony to look for a table (it was difficult, as the restaurant was very busy), it came to my attention that we would be able to see if the boat that we had snuck onto was still there. Sure enough, after we got to our seats, the boat was in plain view. I felt silly at the time I bought my new clothes for a disguise, but after being seated, and in such close proximity to the yacht, I was pleased with the choice I had made. This did make me more certain that the increasing numbers of police officers in sight were around because of the painting, and that Vernon and I may have unwittingly got ourselves involved in a major theft.

To ease my nerves (as I was beginning to feel anxious), I tried downplaying the scale of the situation in my mind, convincing myself that the whole thing wasn't as big as it seemed and that it would harmlessly blow over. This seemed like a bright idea, and I actually felt like I was going to be in for a pleasant afternoon meal. That was until I logged onto the restaurant Wi-Fi and saw that the sighting and disappearance of the painting was one of the main news stories for France, making it on to the homepage of France's main national news website.

After using an app to translate the news story, it appeared that Vernon and I were mentioned as it had our description and everything. What was interesting to me though, was that the news article didn't mention that a painting had been stolen, but rather money! This seemed odd to me, as the painting was clearly gone (maybe the painting had money hidden inside it that we hadn't noticed, or maybe it was involved in some dodgy dealings). This all seemed very suspicious to me.

I did think that the supposed victims shouldn't be too surprised that they were the target of such a high-profile theft. Yes, they probably liked to have the painting on display, yet when mooring up a flashy yacht and visiting a place like Boulogne with limited security, leaving it out in plain view wasn't the brightest idea. To me, it seemed crazy to have that painting up on the wall.

Despite everything that was going on, I thought better of the whole situation that had arisen and decided to enjoy some delicious food that I had ordered. Looking to save my money by going for the cheapest option possible, I ended up getting one of the lowest-priced items on the menu: a cheese sandwich. The sandwich set me back €4, but I guess that since I was paying for the seat as well, the price was slightly more justified than when I was on the ferry. After enjoying the food and getting into some deep discussions about the concept of time, we quietly went back to the coach, trying to keep a low-profile considering what was unearthing near the harbour.

We met up at the coach for the last leg of the trip with no issues – everything went relatively smoothly from here on in. While on the coach I soon noticed that the coverage of the story regarding the stolen painting was only intensifying. Flicking through various news articles, I then got a few messages back from Butch in regards to the painting after I had sent the photos through to him earlier in the day. Since sending him the images I had captured of the front and back of the painting, he had been researching it and was very interested in the connotations of it, and also why the media weren't reporting that the painting was the thing that was stolen.

Butch followed up these messages with one specifically about the map on the back of the painting. It seemed that this not only authenticated the painting as the real one, but was also important in another aspect related to the overarching narrative behind the painting's backstory. Indeed, this was very interesting. To an extent, this perhaps made sense as to why information on the painting's disappearance was not being reported on, to the degree to which I had originally expected.

At this point, I just wanted to sleep, yet for the final part of the trip the coach driver drove us all to a local bowling alley. We only had time for one round, but to be fair to my teachers, they did a pretty good job at fitting a lot of different activities into the itinerary. I wasn't able to engage much in the bowling, as not only was I physically and mentally drained of energy, but I was also messaging Butch and Millie back and forth about their ongoing research on the painting. It was interesting that I had managed to take a picture of the map just before it went missing. Butch and Millie were quite keen about getting involved it travelling to the location of the map, but I wasn't so enthusiastic, as after the happenings of Operation Golden Goal, and the possibility that this could lead to getting involved with some dangerous people, I was more keen on lying low and keeping a low profile over the summer.

Although I took a more casual approach to the bowling, I didn't actually do too badly. In fact, I finished in second place out of our group of six. It's weird, because the score I got was literally my highest one ever. I feel that when I just go out there and don't think about it I do better; it's as if in the past I've been trying 'too hard'.

Here, my approach was to slowly roll the ball down the aisle, aiming to prioritise precision and accuracy over power. The consistency of my precision helped me get a fairly dependable score each round (even though I didn't get a single strike). The person in our group who ultimately won was Connor, who scored either a strike or a spare (even coming up with a turkey) in each and every round.

Vernon's group had an interesting finale, with Vernon and Will going into the final wave tied on points at the top of their group's rankings. Bowling his final bowl of the evening, Vernon only managed to knock seven pins overall meaning that Will only needed to knock down two out of four remaining pins, after he had scored a six with his first bowl. With everyone watching (including all the other people who weren't from our school who had bought into the hype and euphoria that our school was creating), Will nervously stepped up to bowl, lifting his arm back and ready to release the ball. Although he only needed to knock two pins over, it definitely looked easier than it probably was, as the 4 pins were scattered far apart. As the ball was released from Will's unique grip and landed onto the alley floor, it felt as if time significantly slowed down. You would have been able to hear a pin drop if one actually did drop, and that's because along with everyone being so zoned in on the final throw, the people behind the front desk had even agreed to turn off the music for the final round to help Vernon and Will with their concentration.

Anyway, Will's throw was heading straight towards one of the pins. It looked as if he was only going to knock one down. The ball went smack into the pin, before then clipping another pin on its way to the end of the alley. Will had done it! Yet, there were no prizes for the victor, and as we were running slightly late for the ferry, the teachers immediately rushed us all off to the coach.

We then climbed onto the coach, ready for the long journey home back to England. Although not every part of the trip went to plan, it was a pretty awesome experience to travel all the way to a foreign country. With us nearing towards the ferry, I was literally glued to my phone, frequently refreshing various apps for updates on the stolen painting. I was also able to see some of Ricky's vlog that he had just dropped.

Ricky has recently ventured into internet vlogging, and since starting in June, he has managed to amass an average of five hundred regular viewers. His latest video on his day of paintballing was especially impressive, fully capturing the perceived thrill, emotion and intensity he and his comrades would have been experiencing in the midst of the paintballing battle. For parts of the video, I actually felt like I was in the middle of a paintball war myself. Yet I wasn't. I was on a coach that was about to board a ferry back to England. After seeing what a great time Ricky had had with some of my other friends who chose to do paintballing, I began to ponder whether I made the right decision in going to France. I mean, I kind of got myself into a sticky situation, and although it was a thrill to make the getaway from the boat with Vernon unscathed, I felt slightly anxious about the potentially dangerous situation I may have landed myself in.

Anyway, after enjoying the vlog, I habitually did a few swipes and finger presses on my phone to check my messages, seeing if Butch had sent anything. From the start of when I got onto the coach, Butch messaged me saying that he was confident he had something incredible to tell me in relation to the painting's cryptic map, and that the next message I got from him would probably be very important. After constantly checking my phone every ten minutes for about two hours, I decided to leave things be and not bother checking again, especially as my phone was on 2% battery power.

We soon got onto the ferry, and as I was so exhausted, I literally went around it half asleep just looking for somewhere to nod off. All of a sudden nothing else really mattered. I think that some other passengers were experiencing something similar, with sofas (that were actually for the passengers to sit on) being taken up left, right and centre by sleepy people. With my long overdue sleep having to wait till we arrived back in England, Elise and Vernon helped me over to the café/restaurant seating area, as I actually nearly fell asleep while I was walking with them. I was too tired to talk, and so I ended up fitting in a short, but sweet, forty-five minute power nap, while sitting upright. Obviously, it wasn't the most comfortable nap that I had had, yet it was definitely one of the most fulfilling. With the ferry arriving in England, I slowly got onto the coach and immediately went to sleep; not waking up until the coach arrived back at school.

Getting into my dad's car in the school car park, I closed my eyes and literally drifted off straightaway and thankfully it wasn't before long that we arrived at the house. I got ready to go to bed, and although I had slept quite a bit on the return journey, I was still desperate to go to sleep. With the pupils who went on the French trip not having to go into school the next day, as it was a 'rest day', I was free to get up as late (or as early) as I wanted. I had a whole day to fill. With the possibility of an exciting day ahead, I closed my eyes and went to sleep.

CHAPTER 6

The Day Off

Wow. That was a good night's sleep. After spending two nights on a coach it was an exquisite experience to wake up in my own bed, feeling fully refreshed for the free day ahead. Never before had my own bed felt so comfy. After lying in bed for a while, I began to ponder what I was actually going to do with the precious day off school. As strange as it may sound, I actually prefer the night before a day off, than the day off itself. I guess it's because there's this nice feeling where I don't have to worry about anything the next day. When the day itself comes though, I sometimes get bored until I figure out what it is that I want to do.

Finally, I sprung up out of my bed to check the time on my phone – I was shocked. The time was 12:23 p.m., but that wasn't what I was surprised at, as

I had 15 unread messages and 8 missed calls from Butch. Something was up. I thought about calling him, but decided to delay my impulses and be patient in reading through everything that he had initially sent me. My mood calmed though, as after scrolling through the messages I came to the realisation of what the messages were expressly referring to.

Butch had even sent me a flurry of links to articles connected to the missing painting, in addition to some research papers with evidence supporting his claim in relation to his apparent discoveries. Usually I wouldn't know what to make of everything that I was being sent, but after spending roughly two hours spiralling down an internet wormhole based on what Butch had told me, as well as reading and reflecting on what he had told me in correlation with what I had seen and experienced, the ideas and theories began to solidify in my mind, forming a somewhat coherent theory. After digging deep, the overarching narrative of the missing painting was vastly different to what I had first thought after looking at it at face-value.

Looking over and seeing the MegaWay 5 out in the open, I played on it online for a short while, but I soon got bored, as most of my other friends who game with me were at school, finishing off the last part of their activities schedule. As Vernon also came on the trip with me, it would usually be fair to assume that he was interested in going on the MegaWay 5 with me, yet he was instead working on the Verntron 2.0.

To be fair to Vernon, this was at least something worthwhile and exciting while the MegaWay 5's appeal was beginning to wane. After the enthralling adventures that I had been going on, entering into a virtual world on my screen was never going to be as exciting as experiencing something in person.

After thinking about what to do, I did think it'd be cool to work on the Verntron 2.0 (if Vernon would let me), as I was heavily involved in the destruction of the original. Subsequently, after organising a video conference with Millie and Butch for the evening, I texted Vernon to see if he minded me coming over: he didn't.

I later arrived at Vernon's where he was busy at work, constructing his updated and new version of the Verntron. I guess that, although it was devastating for the first version to blow up the way it did, it exposed some potential weak points in the bike, giving Vernon some inspiration for how he can make the bike even better. It was cool watching a genius get to work, and with Vernon showing me the ins and outs of his operation at hand, I soon found myself enthused with excitement for how it was going to come together (even though it was still in the early stages of development). The more Vernon went over the issues with the original bike, the more relieved I was that we had managed to come away from the ride in May without any serious injuries – is was apparent that there were many things that could have gone wrong that didn't.

After we (well, mostly him) had been working on the Verntron 2.0 for a few hours, and after we had had something to eat, I was about to head home for the video conference that we had all organised with Butch and Millie. Yet as Vernon had been on the boat with me, it was probably a good idea to do it with him, and he agreed that it'd be better for us to do it at his place, in his bedroom.

With Vernon on board (and also quite excited), we both invited Elise and Ricky over to join us at the house for the meeting. We weren't sure whether to involve both of them in this, but as we could trust them not to tell the whole school, we thought it would be good to involve them both in the overarching narrative of the situation.

So, I messaged Elise and Ricky regarding the meeting, and within moments a flurry of questions came my way. It became obvious that they were intrigued and exhilarated at the prospect of what was to come. I think that Elise was quite glad to be on board as she was in France when the painting was actually stolen off the boat, while Ricky seemed full of energy after engaging in a second day of paintballing. Elise said she was happy to come over to participate in the video conference, while Ricky said he would come over after it started as he wanted to finish off editing his vlog on his second day of paintballing.

Soon, Elise arrived at the door, and with the meeting about to start, we sat in Vernon's bedroom ready for Butch and Millie to come on the screen. With Butch being in America in the Eastern Time zone, he was about 5 hours or so behind us. I think that he might have just been racing, as he looked all sweaty, while he was still wearing his racing overalls.

The meeting began abruptly with Millie cutting to the chase and breaking down her findings. I tried to keep a straight face when this all went on, as the situation felt like a spymaster giving her superspy agents an outline of their mission briefing. With her having discovered new things since the meeting was organised in the early afternoon, I could immediately tell that things were going to get interesting.

CHAPTER 7

Debrief

Wow. That was an interesting meeting. Because I had been consuming such a vast amount of information, I didn't even notice that Ricky had entered the room to join us.

From the discussion, we came to the conclusion that the painting on the boat was in fact the world-renowned painting, '*Le Frommel*' that had gone missing from an art gallery in Florida about a week before my trip to Boulogne. From comparing the photographs I had taken, with various online sources, including news articles, Butch asserted that he was 97.56% sure (I don't know why he didn't say 99.9% sure - it was as if he had used a computer to calculate how sure he was, which to me doesn't make sense, because how can you actually do that?) that we had taken a picture of the same painting that had been stolen from an art gallery in Florida.

None of us came to a conclusive answer as to how it was stolen in Florida, but we were pretty certain that the group behind its unlawful withdrawal were professionals in this domain. We weren't sure who, but since Vernon noticed that the letters 'FRS' were printed on the side of the yacht, that was what we referred to the group as. I wondered if it stood for initials like 'Fred' 'Rupert' and 'Steve'. However I saw about 4 guys on the boat at least, so I doubted that that was what the letters stood for.

So, as it turned out that the painting had been stolen on the night prior to its scheduled unveiling, we had a theory that the FRS had worked behind the scenes with someone in security on the night of its initial disappearance. This then begged the questions as to why the alleged thieves were in Boulogne-sur-Mer, and who they were as an 'organisation', because the dudes who came after Vernon and I were incredibly aggressive.

Although the conspicuous appearance of the FRS in the broad daylight of Boulogne initially bemused us, Vernon suggested that they could likely have been there to sell the painting (or to do a dodgy dealing related to it). This theory made sense, as what would a crime syndicate do with all the paintings that they stole, other than put them up for sale (unless of course they simply liked the paintings that they stole and didn't just want to pay for them)?

The reason Vernon originally came up with his theory was based on the likelihood of the back of the painting holding a high degree of significance, possibly linking with the reason as to why there was a high demand for it. This made sense to us all, as the map on the back of the painting definitely looked like it had an added dimension to it in regards to its overall presence and appearance. The question is though... who were the two guys who took the painting off the boat, and who were they associated with? This was what intrigued us.

Not only would the group behind the painting's disappearance have the FRS out to get them, but the police also, as well as any other agencies who might be involved in the overall investigation...and of course there would be the Gonzalez family.

The Gonzalez's were actually the rightful owners of the painting, having historic connections with it from the day it was created. With the painting being forgotten about for decades, the Gonzalez family found the painting hidden away in the corner of their attic after a big clear out of their old, historic property that had been in the family for over 100 years at the time. Struggling financially, the sale of the actual house itself was their only hope of paying off a huge sum of debt that had stacked up over several generations.

Although he thought he had found 'just another painting' after noticing it in the corner of the attic, Alberto Gonzalez brought 'Le Frommel' to a painting authentication specialist in case it could be worth a lot of money. After a day of examining the painting, it was confirmed to be one of the lost paintings of the world-renowned artist Enrico Gonzalez. Without previously knowing this, it was from digging further into his family's history that Alberto learned that Enrico was actually his great-grandfather. The painting must have been left behind by Enrico and forgotten about for numerous years! After making this discovery, the family decided to loan the painting to an art museum in Miami, where it would be displayed, providing an increase in tourism to the city.

With the city of Miami planning a special ceremony inside the Miami Tower, security was ramped up for the unveiling of the long-lost painting of Gonzalez. This wasn't surprising considering the painting was valued upwards of $5 million (it's even gone up since).

It was rumoured that the painting was worth more than the sum that the main news outlets were reporting (probably to prevent the attraction of criminal exploitation). Knowing all this, we came to believe that the FRS bribed someone (or several people) on the security team, as they managed to steal the painting during the night before it was to be revealed, subsequently leaving the country without a trace. It seemed strange that the painting was supposedly stolen on the night before the grand unveiling of all nights, with it arguably being the time where the security would be tight and alert to any sign of trouble. Alternatively, Ricky theorised that in a major plot twist, the FRS could have been the security team itself, and were somehow able to bluff their way into the position of security. Either way, the whole thing seemed really fishy.

It would have been a long boat ride to Boulogne for the FRS, but from the calculation of how long it would take to get from Miami to Boulogne on boat, it made sense that they would be in Boulogne at the same time that Vernon, Elise and I were there on our trip. Every part of our theory seemed to fit together like a seatbelt clicking into its socket. I actually find the seatbelt click to be really satisfying, especially when I know that everything is in place and that I am fully ready and prepared for the journey ahead. Click.

With it seemingly conclusive that the FRS were behind the original steal in Miami, we wanted to figure out who the two men that stole the painting on the boat were associated with (and what's really ironic here is that the professionals in stealing, got stolen from themselves, unless they set up some controlled opposition to scatter the police in various directions, like a game of 4D chess).

Towards the end of the meeting we all agreed that the authorities, who were after the FRS, were also probably going to be after the men who stole the painting from the FRS. At the climax of our discussion, I put forward the question as to whether any of us should even get involved, as we had already gone through a lot in the preceding months leading up to this meeting. I really wanted to spend the summer laying low, as Year 10 at school was the going to be the start of my GCSE's. As part of my studies I was going to be doing triple Science and with this I was told by numerous teachers that the workload was going to be very hectic; I needed to be fully refreshed before entering into the next school year.

My preference was tested though after Butch explained the background story of the Gonzalez family, consequently putting me into limbo. Hearing the situation of their family and what they had been through slightly influenced my thinking, giving me good reasons when considering whether to help them. Their family's connection with Miami went back a long way too, with Enrico having an influence behind the city becoming the megacity that it is today, attracting banking investors from all over the place. After learning of the Gonzalez's family history in relation to Miami, we then discovered that the map on the back of the painting exactly resembled a map of Miami! Feint markings on the map also seemingly referred to the Miami Tower, with their being some writing referring to it in Spanish, as well as a small 'x' marked where the Miami Tower is located on the map.

This was very interesting indeed, especially considering that on the night Gonzalez was arrested in Miami, it was at the top of the Miami Tower. With there being rumours that he was about to be arrested at the time, he gathered up his paintings (20 to be exact) and hid them in a secret place that only he knew of. The location of the paintings is still unknown to this day. There have been many theories and news reports written on the whereabouts of these paintings. With their popularity at the time being a significant contributor to making Miami the city that it is today, the value of the paintings continues to rise as each year goes by. It's estimated that the entire collection is worth at least $500 million. I'm not sure how true this is, but since they have been missing for nearly one hundred years, there does seem to be a ring of truth behind it. With the hunt for the paintings continuing, it has been thought that no one has got any nearer to finding the answer to where they are. Although over the years numerous people have claimed to find them, their claims have been repeatedly refuted by archaeologists and experts in authenticating and examining historic artwork.

It was thought that all of the paintings were hidden in the same place, yet a letter was discovered next to where *Le Frommel* was found, affirming that it was the one painting 'to rule them all' (in Spanish). I was sure that I had heard that from somewhere before, but I wasn't sure where. Anyway, in the letter Gonzalez wrote the night before he was arrested, he said that he had hidden his favourite painting in a separate place from all the others. In the same letter Enrico also revealed his innocence, giving a cryptic clue (not revealing everything) behind what had actually happened.

Upon his impending arrest, and after going into hiding for several days, Gonzalez was chased to the top of the Miami Tower. It is thought that this is where he hid his final clue, yet enthusiasts were still unsure of its whereabouts. The letter and the painting found by Alberto was ground-breaking in the search for the paintings, as clues directly relating to Gonzalez had been hard to come by.

Still to this day, historians debate the reasoning behind Gonzalez's arrest. Some say that he was set up for fraud, while others say that he was a mastermind behind a grand money laundering empire. The most accepted narrative was directed towards him being set-up, with there not being any evidence of him actually doing anything wrong.

It has since been well-known that Gonzalez was set-up, and that he didn't actually do anything wrong. The perpetrator, so to speak, was actually a close friend of his who made it look like Gonzalez had killed someone. With this being the case, and Gonzalez's innocence being affirmed, the Miami City Council constructed a statue of him, and also named the biggest art gallery in the city after him. I guess that the saddest part here was that it didn't actually contain any of his most famous works (the twenty-one lost paintings). Wanting to make amends for his wrong imprisonment, the search was heavily funded by the City Council, with this ground-breaking discovery of the letter and the painting in the attic of his old house by Alberto, most likely being the biggest step in the right direction in half a century (and arguably since the paintings were hidden).

Gonzalez was not kept in prison for long though, as he managed to escape within 6 months. After his escape, supposedly no one heard anything of him. It would be interesting to know how long he lived to, as he obviously wasn't still alive, as he would have to be something like 150 years old.

Interestingly, Butch had been in his home state of Florida for the past month, racing cars. One of the reasons he knew so much about Gonzalez and his family was because his younger brother, Monty, was friends with someone from the Gonzalez family (Miguel Gonzalez). Even though I'd never met Monty, Butch says that he had an idea of who I am from the 'goal' I scored at the Capital City Stadium. As clips recorded by some individuals in the crowd of me running onto the pitch and 'scoring' went viral, it wasn't surprising to me when I heard that this was how he knew of me. With Butch having a connection to someone from the Gonzalez family, I was able to see a bigger picture behind the stolen painting and how it did in fact make sense for me to get involved.

Hopeful of us being on board with the mission, and somehow detecting the cogs of careful consideration turning in my mind, Butch explained that we all needed to act swiftly if we were going to have a chance of finding the lost paintings of Miami. It was a race against time, with it being highly likely that there were numerous other organisations in addition to the FRS who were after the lost paintings, arguably making the whole mission very dangerous. With the craftiness of the FRS, we suspected that they would have this in mind; setting up fake decoy trails for the relevant authorities, leading them to inevitable dead-ends. If we were to embark on this, we would have to be ultra-vigilant in every way. As we assumed that the lost paintings were in Miami by looking at the map, the obvious move by the people who stole the painting from the FRS would be to lead as many interested people away from this area (if they recognised that the map was of Miami, which they probably would). It could even be the case that the other paintings might be a start to finding other lost treasure. This painting really was the key: it was the key to Miami.

I kept flip-flopping on whether to go, even though Butch and Millie said having the four of us around would be very helpful in finding the rest of the paintings. Although the one that was initially stolen by the FRS may never be recovered, using the photograph that I had taken, we might be able to find the hiding place for the other twenty before the thieves who stole *Le Frommel* did. We doubted that the FRS would want the other paintings as, although it appeared they were in Boulogne merely to sell the one they stole, we were very unsure of what they knew in relation to the painting's cryptic significance.

The longer I spent considering whether to go, the less enthusiastic I was on the whole idea of going. I mean, America (and in particular Miami), was pretty far away, and I had been looking forward to continuing a new lawn mowing business that I had launched recently. This idea came about after mowing the lawn for my next-door neighbour. For cutting a significant amount of ivy off their fence and mowing their lawn, I was paid £40. As soon as I received the cash in my hand after the hours of hard labour I had put in, I had a lightbulb moment. Ding.

I figured that if I made up a name for my business by doing a quality job and from sending a few leaflets around, I might get some replies asking for more work. However, having only two respondents after three weeks was slightly disappointing to say the least, as I was definitely hoping for at least ten. After speaking to my financial advisor (my sister, Katie, who is about to enrol on A-level Business Studies), I was advised to lower the price to £20. In fact, Katie was very surprised at my original price, saying that she didn't know what was more shocking: the fact that I charged £40 for my services, or that there were some people out there who were willing to pay that much. In my defence though, if I had a lot of money and I was very busy, I might hire me due to convenience. Yet on Katie's advice I realised that she was right – my original pricing strategy was not going to be sustainable in the long term.

So, from looking at the bigger picture, I had a good enough reason to not get involved. Yet, Butch didn't give up on me and still attempted to convince me to come to Miami. He emphasised to me how his younger brother Monty, who goes to school with a member of the Gonzalez family (Miguel), could possibly give us a connection to the treasure's location that no one else would have.

With Monty and Miguel being the same age as me, the possibility of holidaying in Miami with some new friends became appealing, yet I was sure this would be overshadowed by everything to do with uncovering the paintings. If this was just a holiday I would probably go, sit on South Beach, explore the surrounding area and have a good time; but with the possible dangers lurking about and the pressure of everything, I wasn't so sure. However, I still had a nagging feeling in the back of my mind telling me that this would be a missed opportunity if I didn't take it. I was in limbo.

Elise said that she was probably not going to be able to go, as her family had booked a holiday abroad to Spain for a couple of weeks. She said that she might be able to fly over after, but I guess that depends on where we would be in terms of the mission's progress. Ricky was also going to be going away on a whopping four week-long survival camp up in Scotland. This was a big part in his boy scouts training. He said that he had had to go through a lot just to get to this stage, and so he ruled himself out of the trip. With Ricky not coming, and Elise giving us a maybe, Vernon also said that he wouldn't be going, as he wanted to fully focus on the development of the Verntron 2.0.

As the meeting drew to a close, Millie mentioned how she had already booked a flight to join Butch in Florida, who was already in Miami preparing for a major race. She was going, but none of my school friends were. I was in cyclical limbo of what to do.

Well, with Vernon staying and offering me the opportunity to help him with the Verntron 2.0, and with my lawn mowing business having the potential to grow into something special, I knew what I was to do. My family had also booked a really cool holiday for the end of August in Italy. Italy is somewhere I've never been to and I was keen to go there. I really didn't want the Miami mission to drag on until the end of the holiday, causing me to subsequently miss going to Italy.

It looked like it was just going to be Butch and Millie on this one, with all of us having plans. I'm sure that Butch and Millie would solve everything without me – they're more than capable….well, I think they are anyway. I guess time will tell. Besides, I could always go to Miami in the future, but travelling to Italy with my family – that's not something that is always on offer (especially considering that my parents are rarely off work).

Sorry Miami. Maybe another time. With my summer set, good times were to come – I was sure of it.

CHAPTER 8

An Interesting Turn Of Events

It had been a whole week since the dramatic video conference, and I was beginning to wonder whether I had made the right choice in declining the opportunity to help out in Miami. I was still kept in the loop of the events in Miami, and by the sounds of things the mission that Butch and Millie had set out on hadn't really gathered much pace. My lawn mowing business hadn't got off to the start that I was hoping for either, and since slashing the price of my special 'clean sweep' offer down to £20, I had only managed to secure one client asking for my services, and that was my dad.

As the football season had drawn to a close, I appreciated having something productive to do on Saturdays, with the thrills that I used to get from playing on the MegaWay 5 slowly fading away evermore as the days went by.

With Elise and Ricky away, I found myself spending a significant amount of time in Vernon's garage, working on the Verntron 2.0. Even though the original took a very long time to make, Vernon was making relatively rapid progress, as he already had the experience under his belt of constructing the original. From the time spent in the garage, I had already learnt so much about the basics of the mechanical technology involved in the innovation of Vernon's latest creation. It was a privilege to not only assist, but also to witness a cheap and reliable method of future sustainable transportation before my very eyes. Selling a helpful amount of his share of the Kenwright Treasure, Vernon was able to use some of the money for investment in materials, research, and expert advice. The time flew past when we worked on the project together. Time certainly does fly when you're fully engaged in an interesting activity or task (and this was certainly interesting).

Since the Miami meeting, I had been trying my hardest to keep the whole topic of it out of my head, yet it was proving it to be very difficult (partly due to my inquisitive and curious tendencies I have when it comes to subjects of interest). I also get on quite well with Millie and Butch, and I would contact both of them relatively frequently, while I also took an interest in Butch's upcoming Miami race as well. It actually seemed that he would be participating in some big races over in America, with the Miami Premier Race being the first to properly kick-start his string of races in the Florida Race Series.

So, after contacting Millie and Butch the following day, I arrived at Vernon's house to some unexpected news. Vernon told me that was going to be leaving within hours of my arrival to go on holiday for a few weeks with his family. Although I was kind of miffed that he didn't let me know prior to turning up at his house, he only found out himself a few minutes before I arrived. I guess that he was so absorbed on creating the Verntron 2.0 that he wasn't even focused on anything else – and that included his family telling him he had an upcoming holiday with them.

I was gutted. I was looking forward to helping create the Verntron 2.0 over the course of the summer, and for the opportunity to quickly dissolve was hard to take. I still had my struggling lawn mowing business to deal with and attend to, yet this left a big hole in my plans for the summer. The whole thing kind of makes sense though, as Vernon's parents found a really good last-minute deal on the internet for the holiday.

And that's how I found myself all alone in Wiltshire; Miami was calling in the distance. It was as if I was destined to go there. The more I thought about going, the more it made sense. Although there were potential risks and dangers involved with going, not going to Miami could be something that I would end up regretting, for...well...possibly the rest of my life. So, after saying goodbye to Vernon, I let my parents know my intentions. Although they were very much against me going to begin with, I managed to convince them after I reassured them that I would be able to stay at Butch's family house. I immediately messaged Butch and Millie to let them know I had made a U-turn, and after Butch had a brief video call with my parents, telling them that everything was sorted for me to go, they were okay with me going. That was it. I was going no matter what. I was going to Miami.

I then logged onto my computer and began searching for low-priced flights to Miami. After browsing the internet for fifty minutes, the cheapest flight that I could find was going from Hibblesbury Airport to Miami International via JFK for £302!

Once I double-checked to see if this was actually the cheapest flight that I could find, I booked it. In hindsight, this was a little impulsive, but with their only being one seat left on the plane (and the next available flight not until the following weekend), I didn't want to wait around. This was the one: the flight was booked.

The next thing for me to book was a train ticket to get to the airport. For the best price I could find, I would arrive at the airport terminal for 6 p.m. It was cutting it close. Although frantic, things were paradoxically plain sailing as I knew what I needed to do and felt in control of the situation. I went to get a can of cola out the fridge and relax a little, yet there was a niggling feeling in the back of my mind that I had forgotten about something. It was a feeling that I had experienced before. I knew that I had forgotten about something, however, I didn't know what it was.

Since I forgot to hand in my options form for my GCSE's back in February (meaning that I wasn't able to get onto some of the courses that I would have liked), my teacher recommended that I start writing a 'to-do' list on my phone rather than in my school planner. And I have to say that this was brilliant advice by Mrs Marsh. It makes sense that the likelihood of me remembering things would increase, as I literally have my phone on me for most of the time. And to be honest, it is something that I am looking to 'work on' as I definitely think I spend too much time on screens. It's hard not to really. In fact, my phone actually feels like an extension of myself at times. When I don't have it, it's as if there's a physical part of me (like a limb) that is missing. Yes, I know – not good. I think that my screen time is going down gradually though, as for the last 5 weeks, the amount of time I spend on my phone as gone down on average 5% each week. Now that's what I call progress!

Anyway, after taking my first sip of that cola, I went onto my phone to look at my list, and at the top was the thing that I had forgotten about – I still had to mow someone's lawn for my lawn mowing business.

With the airport being one and a half hours away by train, I ideally needed to be finished up some time before catching my train. But with my session booked from 2 p.m., I needed to crack on with mowing the lawn – I was just hoping that Farmer McKeary didn't think I was being lazy once I rushed through mowing his lawn. For sure, this reminded me of Parkinson's Law. In case anyone doesn't know, this is basically well, a law, where the time taken for a task expands in relation to the time given for its completion. This is why I don't like spending too long on something; however, I also didn't want to rush Farmer McKeary's lawn. Before I began to mow, I explained my situation to him and generously he agreed to pay me £20 regardless of when I left, just as long as his lawn was cut. So, after finishing his lawn in just over an hour, I raced back to my house to quickly get ready for a journey to Miami.

I didn't pack too much, as I didn't pay for extra luggage space on the plane while I also had no idea how long I was going to be out there for – it then made me wonder about all the stuff about visas, as the last thing that I would want to happen would be for me to spend time in a Miami jail cell. The more I thought about all this and the rashness of the way I was going, the more some level of anxiety slowly dripped into my mind. Yet, something in me told me to just go with it regardless. So far, Butch's family knew that I was coming and so I was sure that I would be able to sort everything out once I arrived in Miami.

After learning my lesson from missing trains on prominent occasions in the past, I managed to smoothly catch the correct train to the airport in good time. While nervously sitting on the train, I went on to my phone to check for any relevant updates and soon realised that things were getting pretty wild in Miami.

It turned out that the Miami City Library had recently been broken into and trashed. From local eyewitnesses, it was rumoured that the group who broke into it had heavy French accents. From looking at the images that have been caught of the two figures who were directly involved, they bared a very similar resemblance to the two men I saw on the yacht in France. It seemed that the group who had stolen the painting from the FRS in France were after something else...but what?

CHAPTER 9

Arrival In Miami

Regardless of the news, I decided to focus on the positives. I mean, there may be some dangerous people in Miami, but in a way, you could probably say that about most major cities in the world. I ended up sleeping for the most part of the flight to JFK, waking up just as the plane landed. After quickly switching at the airport to catch the flight to Miami International, the reality of the adventure I was embarking on kicked in. I had a good time on the second flight as the seat was a lot more comfortable. With an hour of flying to go, and after ordering a delicious meal from the flight attendant, I watched an episode of *Inspector's Area* to get me through the rest of the journey, as well as watching a bit of *Westminster Warriors' Road to Glory* (a TV series following the success of the Westminster

Warriors football team during the 2017-18 season – a must-watch in my opinion).

The remaining time flew by, and before I knew it, I had arrived in Miami. I collected my luggage, and then got up to step off the plane. As soon as I stepped off, I could feel the difference in climate and overall temperature. The impact of the warm air was similar to the punch that I took from Connor back in May, but it was by no-means painful.

I managed to pick out Butch, and new a face that I hadn't come across before. It was Monty, Butch's younger brother. After a brief welcome, I was invited into Butch's plush, brand-new car. Because Butch is going to be racing in Miami, his team have provided him with a free car. And this car was flashy with all the bells and whistles. It was pretty cool. Butch was driving with Millie 'riding shotgun', while I was in the back of the car with Monty. With us all strapped in, we set off into the night.

Even though it was the middle of the night, there was still a significant level of traffic meaning the journey to the household of Butch's family was one that consisted of a lot of stop-starts. Looking out of the window as we made our way through Miami, I was amazed at the amount of people that were out. Miami certainly seemed to be one of those cities that never sleeps. Simultaneously, I was also astonished at how spacious and big the roads in America are.

After Butch and Millie informed me of what they had been getting up to, I was given some amazing news. It was especially good news for me and I was so pleased that I came over to Miami when I did! Butch explained how he had two tickets to the International Cup of Champions (ICC) Final that was to be played in Miami on Sunday. He explained that as he wasn't really that interested in football, he offered the tickets to Monty and I instead. I was ecstatic because of one of the teams who were going to be participating in the match.

And you guessed it; Westminster Warriors were one of the teams that were playing! I knew about this match, and I had no idea that it was to be hosted in Miami (and if I did know I didn't think that I had a chance of getting a ticket at such late notice). Had I left the decision to come to Miami any later, I probably would have missed this opportunity. My decisiveness was looking like it would pay off.

I was curious as to how (and why) Butch got tickets to such a big match (arguably the biggest annual football match), even though he wasn't particularly interested in football. It turns out that Butch's racing team had a couple of spare tickets available. It was going to be interesting that Monty and I were going together though, as Monty was a big Miami Phoenix fan – both of us were going to be cheering on opposite teams to each other.

Fortunately, I instantly clicked with Monty. I guess that it helped that we were the same age and had similar interests.

I was so hyped for the game. Because Westminster were the Champions of Europe, they were invited to participate with all of the other continental champions. Westminster had managed to reach the final and were the obvious favourites to be crowned the best team on the planet for the first time in their history....and I was going to be there to witness it with my own eyes!

It looked as if Westminster would be facing tough opposition against Miami Phoenix, as they were technically going to be the away side for the game (although the venue was meant to be neutral, but it wasn't because it was being played in Miami). Although a seemingly average team on paper, Miami have been well known to have a pretty solid defence. The main threat when playing them comes through their star player, Bob Smith. If I could sum him up, he's basically the American Roger Jenkins, except he's probably better at dribbling with the ball, but not as good at heading. He recorded a personal high of 46 goals in 28 matches in the American Soccer League for 2017. Although this is impressive, the English Football Division is arguably a lot harder, with a lot of football fans wishing to see him in England, taking an interest in how he'd cope up against some of the more physical teams. Expressing his desire to be loyal to Miami (who pay him $500,000 a week to play for them), it looks like he'll stay there for the rest of his career. With Westminster having the best defensive record in Europe, I was curious as to how Smith would perform in the final. They may as well have titled the match Jenkins vs Smith: Clash of the Titans (although some people would probably think that this was a promotion for a boxing match).

Being filled with excitement, I impulsively sent a direct message to Roger Jenkins, interested in finding out whether he still remembered who I was. I basically just said that I was going to be watching the game and that I was going to be cheering him on. By the time we finally arrived at Butch's house, Jenkins had responded and offered for me to have a signed shirt before the match. What a legend! Taking him up on the offer in response, I was buzzing with excitement for the game. What an event it was going to be!

Stepping into the house, and as Millie was staying in the spare room, I was offered to sleep on the sofa in one of the backrooms. I was so tired that I honestly didn't mind, and was just grateful to have somewhere to lay my head. It was actually a really comfy sofa as well, and with the bed sheets, it felt good.

As well as going to the football game, Monty invited me to meet up with him and some of his friends for the day in Brickell. I know that I was primarily in Miami for the mission, but because I had had such a long journey, Butch said that it would be best if I spent a few days to settle down a bit. In fact, he even said that the whole match would be something to look forward to and take my mind of things. This was still somewhat related to the mission though, as I saw this provided some good opportunities for me to get to know the city better, while also having the chance to make some new friends. Feeling comfortable in my temporary 'bed', I closed my eyes and fell asleep.

CHAPTER 10

Hello Miami

Wow. That was probably one of the best night sleeps that I've ever had. The one after getting back from France was special (and at the time I didn't think that it would be beaten for a while), but somehow this first ever night's sleep in America topped it. And what made it even more impressive was that it was on a sofa. The sun was shining nice and brightly outside – it was a good time to be alive. Looking at the time and realising that I had slept through into the afternoon (meaning that I had missed an informal morning meeting with Butch and Millie) was slightly disappointing at first, but the fact that I hadn't been woken up kind of suggested to me that I wasn't fully expected to attend.

I looked around the room after sitting upright on the couch, and with my tummy rumbling like one of the lawn mowers that I had recently used as part of my mowing business, I got up to find something to eat. I was extremely hungry, while I was also curious as to where everyone else was. Upon walking into the kitchen area, I noticed a note that was left behind. It was from Millie: she had gone out looking for an important clue connected to the location of the painting while Butch was attending a strategic team meeting for his racing team. With the race in Miami less than two and a half days away, he was fully preparing for the Florida Race Series.

I was still hungry and settled for a portion of oatmeal. While eating my delicious hot breakfast, I checked my phone for messages, and it turned out that it didn't really matter that I missed the meeting, as Millie had sent me a message summarising the points that were discussed. We were all still on good terms. Interestingly though, Mille had discovered that Gonzalez wrote about how the secret of *Le Frommel* would 'unlock' the passage to all of his other paintings, in a discovered archived writing, located in the Miami City Library. Although she wasn't sure whether this referred to an actual key, it turned out that Gonzalez had been given a key to the city shortly before his arrest, known as 'The Key to Miami'. She believed that this would unlock the location where the paintings were hidden. So perhaps, the paintings weren't in Miami, but instead the clues lead to the key? All in all, this was hot news.

However, with my excitement geared towards the ICC Final that I had somehow got tickets to (I actually thought that I had dreamt getting the tickets, but after waking up and realising that I was really in Miami, it was clear that it was real), I decided to see what Monty was up to. Coincidentally, I received a text from him at the same moment in time that I was thinking about messaging him, asking if I wanted to meet up with him and a couple of his friends from school. This was an easy decision for me: I was in. Well I thought I was, as just as I was about to send the text to Monty, a message from Millie popped up on my screen. It turned out that she had been doing some important research on the Miami Tower at the library for most of the morning, and with Butch preparing for the upcoming Miami street race, she was desperate for me to go over and have a look at her latest discoveries. This was exciting, and although it would have been cool to hang out with Monty, it became clear to me that going to the library was a priority.

With Miami being a completely brand new place to me, I had no idea which areas were safe/not safe. Judging from the outside, I guessed that we were in a pretty safe area, but from watching an episode of a TV series based in Miami, I reckon that it's pretty hard to tell. But then again, TV shows don't always reflect reality, but just to be on the safe side, I thought it was best not to take too many risks on my first full day in this new city.

As Monty was in Brickell, he told me to meet him there later before heading over to the beach together. Not knowing where anywhere was, the only helping hand I had was my phone, and from simply putting the address of our meeting point into my mapping app, I was able to start my journey. Yes, it probably would be better for me to use more of my own intuition, yet I didn't fancy getting lost at all, and the convenience of it all spoke volumes.

Stepping out into Miami, I was shocked at how big it was. It was very striking how everything was spaced out compared to England, while the differences in wealth of the surrounding areas and neighbourhoods compared to the main inner city proved to be quite telling from the get-go.

The library was about five miles away, and because I was initially quite keen to explore the city on foot, I decided to walk all the way. This was actually quite handy as it gave me a bit of space to think about the possibility of the key being in Miami, while the amble through the numerous neighbourhoods gave me a good opportunity to soak in the atmosphere. On the way to the library Monty sent update messages back and forth regarding the situation and it turned out that he and his friends had decided on doing some surfing. After their session, he suggested for us all to meet up together for food. As he had a football match in the evening at 5:30 p.m., he wasn't going to be eating much, but either way I thought it would be cool to meet new people, while sinking my teeth into some delicious Miami food, so I agreed to meet him later.

Weaving in and around the outer suburbs of the city, I soon found my way near Brickell and close to the Miami River. Seeing that the library was on the other side of the river, I looked around on the map app on my phone for a way over. I found a bridge that brought about a slightly longer detour than I was expecting, but it didn't add many extra minutes onto the journey. Once I encountered this main city library, I had completed half of what I originally set out to do. Next, I needed to figure out Millie's exact whereabouts inside. On the message I had received from her, it said something about 'the archives room'. This seemed simple enough, but if you ever get the chance to visit this library and see the size of it, I'm sure that you'll understand the sheer complexity of the building's layout. It was strange. After looking for twenty minutes around the library and getting lost, I messaged Millie and told her that it was probably best if she came and found me. The only problem with this was that I didn't actually know where I was from that point. I needed to find myself before Millie was able to find me.

I then came across a taped off area, that looked like it had been trashed. It then came to me that this was probably caused by the two guys who had been on the news, mentioned to me while I was on my way to Miami. Perhaps they were looking for the key, based on the clues on the back of the painting. But surely, they should have been looking at the Miami Tower instead?

Eventually, I managed to find the room that Millie had been researching in (I was able to recognise the doorway from an image that she sent me. The only thing was that...she wasn't there. This wasn't a big deal though, as she swiftly came back up after I messaged her again to say where I was. Looking around the room, it was pretty cool to see the layout that Millie had prepared. Somehow, she had managed to 'book' the archives room and set up a little research centre based on now finding the key (which Millie said would inevitably lead to the painting), with the desk and lighting taking up the centre stage of the room. It looked like a whole top-secret operation had been getting underway.

Millie clearly didn't want to lose any momentum on her research and dived straight into the subject matter as soon as she came back into the room. After spending some time examining and zooming in the photograph of the painting that I had taken previously, she showed me something significant that she recognised. It was a symbol of a Phoenix located underneath the word 'key'.

Upon noticing the Phoenix symbol, Mille engaged in further research, seeking to unearth what the significance of this was (or whether it had any at all). She finally came across a document by a historian, who had researched the early modern era of Florida, and located within the research was a section on the symbols of Miami, and their meanings. In case you were wondering, the symbol that resembled the one on the back of the painting consisted of two flamingos, either side of a tall tower. After further inspection we realised how similar it was to the Miami Tower – it had to be the same one!

It turned out that the symbol that was on the map was exactly the same as the one for the original logo for the Miami Art Gallery, started by Gonzalez himself. What made it even more interesting was that there was a key present on the crest as well. After digging deeper, and as this art gallery didn't have a building at the time, Millie discovered that they initially used the Miami Tower to host exhibitions (they still do this once a year as a memento) of the artwork from Gonzalez's time. Everything began to click with what we had previously discovered, and boy was I excited.

All of these findings led her to believe that the key was somewhere in the Miami tower. Whether the paintings were there as well was another question, but we needed to find the exact location of the key first – that was the priority. Personally, I hadn't done any of the brain work in the quest for the key up to this point, and so it was about time that I put some impetus into the quest. I'm more of a practical guy, and so I presumed that the best contribution from me that could reap any kind of reward was to actually go to the Miami Tower itself.

Although we had the probable location, the fact that the tower was so big relative to the size of the small key we were looking for, I didn't step up to the challenge without comprehending the enormity of the task that I planned to undertake. After thinking, and thinking, and thinking, I still had no idea of the specific whereabouts of where the key could be within the tower.

I then pulled up the images that I had taken on my phone, and that's when everything made sense! Looking at the distinct angle that the painting was drawn from, and from watching a vlog of someone who went on a tour of the Miami Tower on the internet, I was able to see that the artwork was painted from the Miami Tower. Obviously I had to be correct in my theory and back it up, but considering the connections that I had made, it did all seem to make sense to me. After doing five minutes of some quick internet research, Millie concurred with what I had proposed.

With this being the most iconic painting (and the personal favourite of Gonzalez's) I constructed a theory that Gonzalez ended up hiding the key near the place that the painting was created and that if we somehow managed to find the exact area that the painting was painted from, we would be able to find a further clue nearby (or even the key itself).

The main reasoning behind my theory came from what Butch told me about Gonzalez when he gave me a lift from the airport. Apparently, Gonzalez etched in his initials into all the places where he painted his paintings. I was fairly confident that this would help us find the real location of the key. We weren't sure what else to do, but the fact that Millie encouraged me to go to the tower with her, to have a look for the painting, filled me with a fair amount of confidence. It was a step in the right direction.

We thought about going over to the tower straight from the library, but because we presumed that it would be packed due to all the extra tourism from the football match that was going to be taking place, we thought that the nature of our quest would be more suited to us going later when there would be less people, while we would also have some time to properly plan out our tower search. However, the fact that I was going to be attending the football match made it somewhat difficult for me to concentrate my efforts on the task in hand.

In the end, we decided that it would actually be better if Millie went while the football game was on, as because this was the biggest game in Miami Phoenix's history, we figured that most of the city's attention would be on the game, acting as the perfect smokescreen for her to enter the tower and have a look around. The only thing that we hoped was that whoever else was around to find the key didn't have the same idea. Butch also wouldn't be able to go, due to his preparation for his race, where he needed to go over various things with his team.

We had spent about an hour going over everything, and with the sun shining brightly outside, I wanted to soak up as much of the Miami weather as possible. I had been inside focusing on this and just wanted to get over to Brickell to meet Monty and his friends. I also invited Millie to come along as well. Thankfully, for the sake of a pleasantly easy stroll to the towering jungle that was Brickell, Monty and his friends had organised to meet up at a place that wasn't too far away from the library. In fact, it wasn't very far away at all.

CHAPTER 11

Burger Basher

The meeting place was at a popular American fast-food chain, *Burger Basher*. As there weren't any *Burger Basher* restaurants back home in England, I was curious about their burgers, but then again, I also just presumed that they might just be the same as the ones in England. I mean, how different can a burger get. A burger's a burger. To be honest, I also found the name 'Burger Basher' to be quite strange. They claim that it comes from the workers bashing the burgers with their fist to make the special flavouring that they sprinkle on top, properly embed into the top layer of the burger. Another theory was that the creator of the business, Bob Beasley, was involved in an accident where he bashed his head on his sink, causing him to slip over. Apparently after waking up, he thought of the idea for the secret flavouring for *Burger Basher* that makes their burgers distinct from all their competitors. Another theory that I found online said that it was chosen because it sounded cool to Beasley and rolled off the tongue well. I'm honestly not sure which one is true, but in a way it could technically be all three, so I think I'll pass when it comes to figuring out which theory the name originates from.

So, we soon arrived at the restaurant, and from the looks of things, it seemed that Monty and his two friends had had a good time surfing. They had already ordered their food, which I was okay with to be honest, but I did find the restaurant to be quite busy, and this wasn't surprising considering that there was a big match involving Westminster Warriors on the way. I did feel at home with there being a few Westminster Warriors fans in the restaurant, noticing quite a few replica shirts. I was kind of glad that there was a queue as it gave me time to think about what I could order. Yes, I get that it is simple to order a burger, yet in the *Burger Basher* restaurant I was shocked at the variety in the burgers. I mean, how can you come up with 33 different types? I was impressed by the creativity on display too. What made it more interesting was that the most expensive burger cost $14.99! I don't know what this is in British pounds, but to me that level of pricing still seemed crazy!

Something that still triggers a small amount of anxiety within is when I suddenly find myself at the front of a queue to order something...before I know what I want to order. Some people that I have spoken to have tried to convince me that a broad choice is a good thing, but if you're as indecisive as I sometimes am, choosing what you actually want can be very tricky.

This occurred when I abruptly found myself at the front of the queue. I was so fascinated at all the different names for the different types of burgers, and also gobsmacked at some of the prices, that it wasn't until Millie interrupting my thoughts, telling me that it was my turn, that I realised I needed to give my order. Not knowing what to have (and also feeling pressured to order quickly, as there was a long queue of presumably hungry people behind me), I literally just asked the guy behind the counter for a burger. After looking at me as if I was deliberately joking around, he asked me "what type" I would like. I literally didn't know, so I just ordered the 'Basheroo'. As this was the burger plastered on posters all around the restaurant, I presumed that this was the common choice, and therefore the safest out of the 33 different options. When I ordered, the guy looked a bit surprised, and it wasn't until I was given the receipt that I figured out why. It turns out that, not only is the 'Basheroo' one of the spiciest burgers, but it's also the burger that was the most expensive (yes, the one that cost $14.99).

This was rather embarrassing, as I gave myself a tight budget for this trip, and $14.99 on a burger didn't really seem that justifiable. Not wanting to be awkward, I just payed up as if I already knew that the burger cost that much when in reality I was just trying to work out how much money I had already spent since being in Miami. In hindsight, I probably should have just ordered the same as Millie (She chose a double-cheeseburger – and yes, you could argue that it was quite boring considering the other options that were available, yet it only set her back $3.99, which is cheap considering I spent about $15 on a similar meal).

With myself and Millie's burgers prepared, we collected them and joined Monty, Miguel, and Julia (a friend of Monty and Miguel) at the table near the back of the restaurant. I tried to be as discrete as possible when it came to my choice of burger, but from the way they looked at my 'Basheroo', I figured that they knew I had ordered the most expensive one. Although this burger was actually the tastiest burger I'd ever had (but it was still not worth the $14.99 that I'd spent on it), I tried to steer attention away from my burger due to the mild embarrassment I was feeling from ordering it.

I didn't need to put much effort into diverting any attention though, as after a brief awkward silence where everyone was looking at the size of my burger, a natural conversation grew concerning a football match that Monty and Miguel were having for their local team, the Brickell Bears. The Bears actually had a decent professional first team, playing in the division below Miami Phoenix. So, it was probably a lot higher standard than the games I had been playing in for Kettleston. But why was their nickname 'Bears'? I often ask myself why sports teams in America generally have a team name associated with an animal or something that expresses positive attributes or dominance. In England, it's very different. Yes there are some teams that have similar names (such as Westminster Warriors), but for football it's usually Athletic, Rover, United, City, or simply 'FC' (or if you play for Nottingham Friday, a day of the week, which I personally find bizarre).

Hearing from Monty, this match was also significantly different from the ones that I would play in England, due to the fact that the home 'stadium' of the Brickell Bears youth teams is on a rooftop of a skyscraper (known as the Rooftop Arena)! Apparently, this was because the club wanted to keep their team in Brickell, but there wasn't enough space. Although the design of the stadium was originally a compromise, the attention it has brought the club sounds like it all ultimately worked out in their favour, with more spectators paying to attend the games than would probably otherwise be the case if they played in a standard stadium.

I'd seen images of these types of football pitches on the internet, and playing on one was something that I had wanted to do. The only concern I had was in regards to the ball being kicked off the pitch – what would happen if someone was in the wrong place at the wrong time on the streets below? I knew that they had a high fence... but still.

Originally, it was planned that I would be shown around some parts of the city before going to watch the match with Millie and Julia, yet I soon discovered that Miguel had somehow injured his ankle from falling over after he had finished his surfing session, meaning that he was ruled out of the match. Miguel and Monty had both been on their phone since, looking for someone to take his place, but on such short notice they were struggling to find someone to fill in. The match itself was nearly cancelled with the Bears struggling for a starting XI. Not wanting to forfeit the match, and with a playoff place slipping away, the coaches both agreed for the match to go ahead irrespective of the situation.

From the direction that the conversation was going, it seemed pretty obvious that Monty and Miguel wanted me to play. Without hesitation I volunteered myself to step in. Monty quickly messaged his team, and it seemed that they were all happy to have me in on board. I was buzzing. This also made going around Miami a bit more purposeful, as I needed to find myself some football boots that fitted. This game was probably only going to be a one-off and so I wasn't bothered about the quality of the boots - I just needed a pair.

Walking around Brickell first-hand was an amazing experience. The sheer size of everything made my jaw drop frequently, and after picking up some football boots, as well as a few souvenirs, the time to meet up for the match crept up on us. It was nearly game time. The five of us then journeyed our way over to the Rooftop Arena to meet up for the game.

Actually getting to the football pitch was a surreal experience to me. When preparing for a football match back in England, I'd usually already be dressed in my football kit, before stepping out of the car and then walking from the car park to the football pitch that was normally in the middle of a local playing field. Yet this time, the teams met in dressing rooms that were near the top floor of a skyscraper in the middle of Miami. The fact that we were probably going to have a proper tactics board in the dressing room made me even more excited for the game! Honestly, stepping into the elevator to make my way to the stadium felt so cool. With other people coming with me, I felt like a fighter who was walking to the ring with an entourage of support. This was thrilling!

We arrived slightly late, but as I was desperately needed for the game, the coach let my lateness slide, and by his attitude it was as if he was apologising to me - I guess that he was just very appreciative that I could play considering the desperate situation his team had found themselves in. After slipping on my kit in the dressing room, I joined Monty and the rest of the team outside to do a pre-match warm-up. I was going to be playing as a central midfield player, with this being Miguel's usual position. Training with the team, I was surprised at how good everyone was. I felt like an imposter at times. Judging from the warm-up drills, I already had the impression that the standard of the game was going to be much higher than that of the Kettleston matches I was used to playing in. Just by training with the players, they all seemed faster, stronger, and a lot more skilful than the level I was used to. Although I felt slightly intimidated, I was sure that playing with these players would improve me as a player.

Kick-off loomed and with 5 minutes to go before we were all set to start, I was sitting there in the dressing room, wearing a spare Bears kit that had different shirt sponsors to everyone else on. I listened to the tactical team talk by the coach, and it was a lot more advanced than what I was used to from my playing experience in England. Although I didn't understand a lot of what the coach's tactics were, I reckon that all of the other players were probably used to the masterclass that I was hearing. I was hoping that I would get to grips with the style of play that the team was used to implementing.

This was an important match for the team though, as they needed to finish in the top eight places of their league to make the playoffs. They still had plenty of games left, but being on a three game losing streak, and playing the team that was at the top of the table, they were in danger of dropping out of the playoff positions for the first time in the season.

Walking out onto the pitch, I was surprised at the number of spectators in attendance. Don't get me wrong, there probably weren't more than a hundred people watching, but for an under 14's game I didn't think that this sort of game would be that interesting to watch. The team had a surprisingly big following. The American national anthem then played after we had lined up together as a team. It was then time for kick-off!

The game got off to an interesting start from the get-go. The ball got booted out of the stadium with the first kick of the game after the opposition team's striker attempted to score from the half-way line straight from kick-off. I found myself hoping that the ball didn't land on someone below, as a ball travelling down onto the street from the height that we were playing at would be very dangerous indeed.

After this misplaced attempt from the opposition, the rest of the half played out in a relatively quiet manner. The only real highlight of the half was from a penalty kick for the opposition team. Disappointingly, this all came about from an accidental handball by me. Even though I'm not one of the tallest players on the pitch (I'm probably in the middle), our team captain, Ryan, said that I should be in the wall for a free-kick. This seemed fine to me at first, but after comprehending how close I was in proximity to a ball that was about to be struck towards me, a whirl of fear emerged. Their player stepped up and took his shot. The ball was fired towards me, and from a reflex reaction, I raised my hand to stop the ball from hitting me flush in the face. The ball hit my hand and that was it. The referee called for a penalty kick. I felt awful. The player who had earlier kicked the ball out of the stadium stepped up to take it. I wasn't sure what to expect from this player, as he had also had another shot from about 30 yards out that nearly went out of the stadium to join the other ball that he had kicked out earlier. I was sure that these misses were a minor blip that would be corrected once he took the penalty, but no, he blazed the ball over the bar, and in the process managed to kick another ball out of the stadium. I actually felt bad for him, but I was also relieved that my handball didn't lead to a goal going against us. At half-time the score was 0-0.

Entering the changing room, I felt a bit embarrassed about my subdued performance, but this was somewhat hidden due to the overall poor display from the team collectively. We hadn't been good enough. Feeling downcast, a thought came into my head that invigorated me with a spark of confidence: I couldn't be substituted off, and therefore I had nothing to lose. I needed to take more risks in my play.

In terms of tactics, I continually struggled to actually take in much of what the coach was saying. I zoned out. The only part of the team talk that I remembered was when he mentioned my name, and that's when he caught my attention. He basically just told me to "run in behind" the defender. I just nodded my head trying to make out that I understood what he was asking of me, when in fact I didn't have a clue what he was on about. Like I've said before, all I think about in regards to football is to score goals. It's that simple.

We walked back out for the second half and within forty seconds of the restart we formed our first major attack. It all stemmed from, in my opinion, our best player in Harrison. He literally received the ball after the kick-off for the second half and dribbled past the entire opposition defence. He then found himself 1-on-1 vs the goalkeeper. It looked as if he was going to shoot and score a fantastic solo effort, yet instead he feinted to shoot and ran around the keeper, giving him an open goal. He then did a 'no-look' shot, and unfortunately dragged the ball wide of the far post. It was an unfortunate miss.

The game continued, and for the next twenty or so minutes after this, we dominated possession and had plenty of chances to score, yet we were still struggling to breach the opposition defence. Our best chance fell to me of all people. I was on the edge of the penalty area and played a neat 1-2 pass with Monty. I found myself in a good position inside the area, but on the half-volley I completely ballooned the ball over the bar.

With our team completely dominating and pressing for the winner, it looked as if the game was going to end in a draw. This game had a lot of similarities to the last game that I played for Kettleston back when we got relegated in May, apart from this time around I was way more exhausted. The intensity was on another level, and although it helped being surrounded by quality players, having to keep up was tough. With one minute to go in the match, Harrison picked up the ball on the left hand side of the pitch. He then cut inside onto his right foot and whipped in a delightful ball. It was a really tough ball for the defenders to handle. Monty was in a good position to head the ball, and got a small flick on the ball. Yet, it wasn't enough to divert the ball home. Fortunately I managed to anticipate the trajectory of the ball and stretched my foot out as it came towards me. I got a touch onto the ball to divert it towards the top-corner of the goal. The opposition goalkeeper was rooted to his spot as the ball flew into the back of the net. It was a postage stamp finish. 1-0 to Brickell Bears.

When the ball went in, the Rooftop Arena erupted. Our team was so happy. It looked like we had won the match right there at that moment. Miguel even came over and joined in on the celebrations, before being immediately sent back to the stands by the referee. One of their players took offence at Miguel's behaviour and came over to swing a punch at him. A huge brawl looked like it was going to emerge, with nearly all twenty-two players on the pitch (plus Miguel before he went back to the stands) trying to break up a few of the players who wanted to fight. In the end, nobody got hurt, but three players did get sent off, in addition to four players being shown yellow cards.

After the chaos that had ensued eventually calmed down, the game restarted with the opposition team kicking off. I thought that the game was over, but another twist came about when their striker took on a shot from kick-off. I don't think that our keeper was expecting the shot (especially as the same striker had already kicked two balls out of the stadium), as it took him about a second to react. By the time he reacted, the ball looked like it was going to loop over his head and into the back of our goal. The ball hit the crossbar and then bounced out for a goal kick to us. From the goal kick, our keeper then kicked the ball up the pitch, and then that was that; the referee blew the full-time whistle - we had won!

After the game, Monty and I went over to the stands to see Miguel, Julia and Millie. Miguel in particular was really pleased to see me, giving plaudits for my performance. It was great to receive acclaim from one of the team's best players, but in all honesty I was just glad that I was able to play at such a high standard. Julia and Millie also congratulated me on my goal which was encouraging.

After shaking hands with the opposing team, we all walked back into the dressing room. Generally speaking, we were all mostly on good terms. Everything had calmed down which was nice to see, however after looking at the time on my phone, I quickly informed Monty. We then both notified the coach and the team that we would be heading off, which they were fine with. We may have been missing out on a team meal after the game, but there was something that Julia had lined up for us that was probably more exciting to say the least.

Just before leaving, the coach invited me to train with this team whenever I was around in Miami, also giving me a card with his contact details on. This was pretty cool, and gave me something to think about going into the football season. What if my future was in Miami after all? I mean, after a day I had already fitted in to the city quite snuggly. It felt like the place for me, and with an opportunity to explore the nearby sea, the 'Miami Mission' was just getting better and better.

Monty and I changed out of our football kits and were soon ready to leave with the rest of the crew. We entered the lift, and with the pitch being on top of a tall skyscraper, I had forgotten how long it took for us to get to the top of the building as it felt like an age before we finally reached the bottom.

In the lift Julia said that through texting her uncle during the match, he had agreed to take us all on a ride in his really cool boat that was moored nearby. This was perfect, as it would give us all a chance to calm down from the match and see the city landscape of Miami from a new perspective. Getting out of the lift, the five of us headed down to meet up with Julia's uncle, Brian, to have a ride on his boat. I just hoped that it was a better experience than the last time I went on a boat prior to this. I was still looking forward to it nonetheless. Miami called, and I was certainly there to answer.

Julia then led the way to her uncle's boat, who had agreed to meet us nearby in the harbour area. Julia played down the size of the boat, not wanting any of us to have too high expectations, which was understandable, I guess.

CHAPTER 12

Boat Ride

It was a wonderful Saturday evening that had been sweetened by the goal that I had scored at the match. For sure, it would be a day that would live long in my memory. We stepped out of the lift and into the foyer area of the skyscraper, ready to embrace the Miami air once again. We were walking down the road when Monty, who was leading the way, abruptly came to a standstill.

At first, I wasn't too sure why this was, but after looking at the car he was intently observing with great astonishment, events from the previous two hours dramatically came full circle: the sports car (that looked like it was worth $700,000) had two smashed windows. I'd seen a few cars like this over the course of my life, but it surprised me that someone would take time out of their day to vandalise someone else's property in broad daylight.

However, it turned out that Monty and I had actually been indirectly involved, as inside the car we noticed two footballs that were the exact same brand as the one's we used for the match that we had just played in – both of their striker's shots must have hit the same car! Now that is unfortunate. If I hadn't given away that penalty, the car probably would have only one smashed window instead of two. It's amazing how someone's actions can affect other people's lives without initially realising!

I'm by no means a philosopher, but comprehending this did put me into a trance, and while thinking about this I nearly stepped into the road, narrowly avoiding getting hit by another car, but thanks to Miguel, yanking me back, the oncoming jumbo car brushed my t-shirt. Phew. And thanks Miguel watching out for me – you're a legend!

I was a lot more careful from here on in, and I think this is a helpful example of how quickly everything can change. I grew in vigilance. After what seemed like a few zig-zags around the concrete jungle of Brickell, I was able to see the ocean in all its splendour. Just across from us was the harbour. There were a load of yachts parked up, and I was there thinking that Julia had tried to downplay the fact that we were all going to be having a ride on a luxurious yacht.

We passed yacht after yacht and after going by each one I was thinking 'this is the one', but that one never came. We eventually walked past all of the yachts, coming across the smaller boats. Okay, I then understood that Julia wasn't trying to downplay expectations – she was just being honest with us. We then got to the end of the row, and came across this small little boat with a red canopy. Looking at it, it was clear that it would possibly be a tight squeeze for six of us to squeeze into. In the end, I was just grateful that we had a free ride. Julia's uncle, Brian, then came out of a little hut on the side of the harbour, next to the boat. The hut was about the size of two portaloos put side-by-side, but the appearance of the business headquarters still looked professional. It turned out that Brian had actually closed his boat-ride business early for the day, to give all of us a ride for free, which was pretty cool.

Anyway, Brian saw the five of us coming and was quick to greet us. After introducing himself, Millie and I discovered something that Brian had in common with me – he was also English. This probably explained why the boat had a British flag printed on the front of it. The boat was also made in England, and according to Brian, he rode on the boat all the way from England to Miami in 2006 for charity. Brian actually owned the boat and lent it out for rides. The cheap price that he offered was a key factor behind the success of his business, while the story of his ride from England in the boat also drew interested customers, actually contributing to him attracting new tourists year after year. He's never left America since. After asking about some key tips in starting a business, Brian told me that if you want to make a successful product or service, it's important to have a story to go with it - it apparently connects the emotions of the buyer to what you are trying to sell them.

During his transatlantic boat trip, Brian actually nearly died from sunstroke and dehydration. Arriving in Miami, onlookers really thought he was dead, but somehow he made a miraculous recovery. I had no idea, but after searching about it on the internet, everything about the boat trip all seemed to be true with there being quite a few news articles on it from 2006, reporting how 'Brian Howard had sailed from Penzance to Miami, raising £100,000 for charity'. It was definitely the same boat: it had history.

Having the backstory to the boat actually helped kick-start the business and since then (apart from a nervy time from 2007-2008), the business has been doing fine. Also, there was a time when the business nearly had to close down due to Brian forgetting to give the customers life jackets on one particular outing - someone fell off the boat and nearly drowned. It really surprised me that the business survived something like that. Maybe he has 'helpful' connections, or perhaps the person who nearly drowned didn't report it. Either way, his business was still around.

After Brian had introduced himself, we got down to business. Brian showed us the boat and went through all the cautions and proceedings that he knew off by heart. As Julia had already been on the boat numerous times with Miguel and Monty, they were able to help navigate and show us around some really cool spots around the areas surrounding Miami.

Although it was still in the evening, the sun was out, and the red canopy actually made out for a cool ride. We got out to a deep point, and all of us apart from Miguel (who still had an injured ankle) went for a swim. I wasn't sure if there were any dangerous species of sea life or if it was 'okay' to swim out where we were, but as everyone seemingly thought it was fine, I just assumed that it was safe. We weren't too far out from land, and there were a few others swimming. After I had done a few jumps into the sea, something caught the corner of my eye from a distance (and no, it wasn't an ice cream van). It was a yacht, but what made it more distinct was that it looked very similar to the one that I came across back in France. It was too difficult for me to tell whether it was the same one, and so I swiftly convinced myself that it wasn't – I was not in the mood to think about having to possibly avoid the FRS again.

After some more swimming, the sunlight theatrically began to dim. We had been out for a while and it was beginning to get late. I think that Brian had enjoyed our company, as after we got back to his shed he invited us all to have dinner with him at a five start restaurant nearby. It was called the *Palm Tree*. To me, it sounded like the name of an English seaside pub, but it was a really popular restaurant with a balcony overlooking the waters. As it was busy, there was a high chance that we would have to book a table before turning up. And we did –managing to claim the last booking for 8 p.m. What a treat! After the tough year I had had, I thought I deserved this.

On the way back, I mentally examined the structural design of Brian's boat, and Vernon and his inventions came to mind. From looking at the size and shape of it, I did in fact believe that it had the potential for a special motor engine to be fitted onto it, similar to Vernon's plans for the Verntron 2.0. I was confident that this could maybe be a good idea for him to think about in the future. I wasn't sure what it could be called though. Maybe the Vernboat?

Our reservation for the *Palm Tree* was confirmed via text, with the six of us then heading straight to the restaurant. We'd hoped that our clothes would dry out quickly in the hot weather and mine had partially, although I was still slightly uncomfortable. We had a nice meal together anyway, and I tried my best to divert any sort of discussion from The Key to Miami, as I wasn't sure whether it would be wise to let Brian in on it after only just meeting him. I mean, although he's Julia's uncle, I didn't know him that well. I think that Millie was thinking the same, as she didn't come close to bringing it up when discussing why she was in Miami.

Instead our conversation steered towards the race that Butch was going to be participating in. He had one of the slowest cars on the starting grid, but in motor racing there's always a chance to get a decent result as long as you go all the way to the end.

The time flew by and after I had finished my portion of a delicious, mouth-watering, Miami Muffin Special, it was 10 p.m. That was enough for me. I was tired, and with there being a possibility that Millie and I were going to be exploring the Miami Tower the following day, I went back to Monty's house to get some sleep.

CHAPTER 13

The Race

I woke up. It was Sunday morning, and with the rest of
the house going to a local church service, I decided to
go along as well. The church was a lot different to the
one that I usually attend back in England. To start off
with, it was a huge cathedral-like building, with
magnificent artwork that really brought the place to
life. There were also about three hundred people in
attendance. This was way different to England, as we
would usually have a similar service in a village hall at
the one I usually went to, with a maximum of about
fifty people. Either way, a church service is a church
service and it gave me a chance to take a step back
from everything that had happened in the 48 hours
prior, and focus my attention elsewhere. Coming out
of the service I felt rejuvenated, ready to tackle the
day ahead.

I'm not really a fan of motor racing. To me it's incredibly repetitive and boring, and there doesn't seem to be much difference to it than watching people run around in circles (in fact, it's basically the same except the competitors are sitting in cars instead of being on foot). I get that it's probably thrilling if you're in the car itself, but as a spectator who only gets to sit at one point of the track, it can be quite frustrating only being able to see a small part of the race at a time? Despite all of this, the main reason that I decided to go was to support Butch in his big race, and to me that was a good enough reason.

For this day, Monty and I decided to travel using a pair of bikes that we found at the back of the garage early in the morning. They were quite flimsy and old, with the seating having to be readjusted on mine every two minutes: It kept drooping downwards, causing me to slide forwards into a very uncomfortable position. As soon as we came across a bike shop in town, we stopped by to get it looked at. The guy at the shop was able to fix it, but after another couple of miles of cycling, the drooping seat frustratingly came back. To counter it, I tried to cycle standing up as much as I could. I did need a rest every now and then, but I'd say that this method mostly worked.

Anyway, we soon arrived at the temporary circuit for the race, which was actually set out on the streets of Miami, taking drivers near the sea. Aesthetically, it was stunning, but when it came to actual racing, previous showings had shown it to be pretty dull. I mean, the streets were very narrow, relative to the cars, so it's no wonder that it's rare to witness an overtake in this particular race – it's more of a high-speed procession. Nonetheless, I'm sure that Butch would be very appreciative of the support whilst whizzing through the streets of Miami at over one hundred and fifty miles per hour.

Although the race was taking place far away from Phoenix Stadium, the fact that the streets were closed on one of the busiest weekends of the year for Miami wasn't the best organisation I had seen. Let's just say that I was glad that we had chosen to use bikes rather than any different mode of transport to get from the church to the race.

Being guests of Butch, we had passes to get us into his team's paddock area. This was pretty cool as it gave us access to what really goes on behind the scenes on race day. Butch briefly came over to us, asking how we were. Millie was also there. It was strange seeing Butch fully focused, dressed in his racing gear. He was wearing his overalls and was like a completely different person, in that he seemed very absorbed on the race. As Monty and I both arrived late we only managed to catch up with Butch for a few minutes before the race was scheduled to begin. Out of 22 cars, Butch was starting in 15th place. We were allowed to stay in the paddock to watch the race, but because our view was so obscured, we decided to go to one of the stands. Having all-access passes, we were still allowed back into the paddock area at the end of the race. I was hoping to go back later to congratulate Butch on a Miami Premier Race win, but starting in 15th place on a circuit that's notoriously hard to overtake on, this looked very unlikely.

The race soon began, and what a spectacle it was. Around the first corner the tyre from the 1st placed car burst, causing him to crash into the barriers. Other cars then spun and collided resulting in a significant amount of debris on the track and numerous retirements. As there was so much debris to clear up. The race was stopped, and with six drivers who were near the front of the grid having to pull out of the race, Butch somehow found himself up to 9th place on the restart. We had to wait around for another forty-five minutes before the race continued again, and so Monty and I made sure to get the most out of our special passes, and went back to Butch's paddock area while the track was being cleared. The six cars that were out of the race were considered to be some of the faster ones and so Butch's team were quietly confident of a top ten finish.

The forty-five minutes were soon over and it was then time to race again. Butch got off to good start again from here, and after the first corner he found himself in 8th place after overtaking a car. As the circuit was one of the shortest for the World Racing League calendar, there were 58 laps (reduced from 71 because of the crash) for the cars to get through.

After 35 laps, Butch had managed to rise up to 6th place. With this being Butch's first ever race at this level (he had only previously raced at two levels below this before, but was only called up because many other reserve drivers were unavailable), it was hard to tell what a 'good' finish would be for him when considering the car that he was in. I looked on my phone and the best a driver from the team had previously finished in the season was 8th place. Although he had a helping hand with six cars retiring at the start of the race, Butch was putting on an exceptional showing. This was all good, and I was happy for him, but with the cars going round and round and round, I actually managed to drift off in mild nap after about forty laps had gone by. I woke up and I was immediately surprised when I discovered that there was a race on for 1st place. Butch had managed to somehow find himself leading the race in

1st place. While everyone else had pitted for new tyres, Butch's team opted to stay out, meaning that he was ahead on the track. Because it then rained, everyone had to pit again, giving Butch a lot of extra time. There were only two laps left and it looked inevitable that Butch was going to take the win. Unbelievable!

There was another twist up ahead though, as the strategy for Butch to stay out on his older set of tyres was suddenly challenged, as the surface of the front left tyre split with half a lap to go, significantly slowing his car down. I think this massively distilled belief in the drivers behind as it looked like they were speeding through the field at a faster rate than they had been going in previous laps. Another one of Butch's tyres then burst, resulting in sparks from two different wheels on his car. At this point it looked like he would do well to just finish the race. Butch was going full throttle though and wasn't ready to give up just yet. On the last straight, he was overtaken by two cars, putting him into 3rd place. The 4th placed car was hot on his bumper, but somehow Butch found an extra ounce of speed to take his car over the line in front, beating the 4th placed car, Terry Marshall, by 0.008 seconds. It looked like the other car finished in front, but the official time had recorded that Butch finished ahead by a very fine margin. What a result.

Butch was on the podium and found himself with a 3rd place trophy for his efforts. Not a bad first race in the Florida Race Series. Well done Butch!

After things calmed down, I reflected on the events of the final lap that had just unfolded before my eyes, and I was pretty sure that I had seen a similar scenario play out on a movie I had seen when I was younger. I can't remember what the film was called, put it was a dramatic finish for the race in the end, resulting in a tie between multiple participants of the race.

I met Butch after and congratulated him. What a race that was. He told me that when it came to the mission, he wouldn't be able to put much time and effort into it over the forthcoming days, due to some of his duties in relation to the racing. I understood, and was happy for him. Mille would still be around to lead the charge for us though. All things considered, it was an afternoon well spent.

Butch was busy, and once the crowd that had gathered for the podium celebrations had begun to disperse. Butch's busyness was evident from the many post-race interviews with enthusiastic journalists that he had to participate in. I was hoping that his new found fame wouldn't make it more difficult for him to come on more quests with the crew in the future.

Running on foot, Monty and I then decided to get out as soon as we could, trying our best to avoid bumping into people on the way out of the temporary street circuit. I hoped that our bikes hadn't been stolen though. I was fairly confident that they would be fine, especially as the one that I rode wasn't exactly the best bike in the world.

Monty and I were doing our best to weave in and out of the crowd of people, and then I bumped into another dude. He was a pretty big guy as well, and as soon as he turned around to face me while I was on the floor, I immediately recognised him from somewhere before. France! I think he recognised me as well, as his face turned from an expression of friendliness to one of sheer rage. I think Monty knew that something wasn't right, as he was already running away. Without another moment going by, I scrambled off the floor, picked up my wallet that I had dropped, and after dodging his attempt at grabbing me, I legged it. I looked behind and could see that he had ordered his entourage of three to come after myself and Monty. The fact that he was in the city was kind of scary, and it was therefore probable that the yacht that I saw on the previous night was in fact the same one that was in France. Everything came full circle again, and I really wasn't too enthusiastic about the prospect of that!

It was actually helpful that there were a load of people, as I didn't feel confident in outrunning the three other guys. Partly making my way through a large crowd of people that were filtering out of the gates, I crouched down to tie my shoes for about a minute. I think this worked, with the three guys who were after me running straight past me, about 15 ft. or so to my left. I hoped that there wasn't anyone else who I knew of at the race, and to make sure that the dude didn't catch up with me again, I did in fact contemplate whether to continue on by crouching down as low as possible (basically by crawling). I was also slightly worried about Monty, hoping that he was alright. I didn't want to return to Butch, as if he was compromised (by them knowing he was involved in the mission), it wouldn't surprise me if they tried to sabotage his car for future races (or something like that).

Wading through the crowd for a few more minutes, I came across a merchandise stand, selling hats. Getting a hat seemed like a good idea. I mean, if they were looking for a fourteen year-old kid who was hatless, how would they spot me if I was wearing a hat? Unfortunately the three of them unwittingly anticipated this next move, as after crawling through some of the crowd of people, I crept up to the hat stand and noticed the three guys standing there on the lookout. Quickly I made a run for it, but in hindsight it probably would have been a more clever 'chess move' if I quietly walked away, with the unusual activity of someone running likely to catch the attention of the three bandits. Once they saw me, the chase was back on!

It was make-or-break time. I darted for the bike station as quickly as I could go, trying my best not to crash into another person. Darting through the crowd, I was like an all-star rugby player who manoeuvred his way through the helpless field. The try line was in sight now, and thankfully Monty had made it there. By the looks of things, he was ready to go and had even unlocked my bike for me. The three dangerous men were on my tail and sensibly Monty had already slowly begun to get his bike into motion. Then, all in one move, like a superspy who was teaming up with his sidekick, Monty tossed me my helmet, as I moved onto the saddle of my bike before I then got into gear, put my helmet on, and cycled off. Whoosh.

The gang of men (probably from the FRS) hadn't given up, and it was no surprise considering that we hadn't got up to top speed. There was a lot of traffic up ahead, and I didn't know whether we could make it before the traffic light ahead turned red. We made it, but that didn't stop the bandits continuing their chase after us, with them speeding through a red-light causing mayhem behind. Finally, after turning into the Miami Gardens through two right turns, we lost them, but just to make sure, we continued riding and took refuge at the top floor of a four storey shopping centre near where we had played the match for Brickell Bears the previous day. Whatever we did, we didn't want to lead them back to where we lived, and being in a shopping centre gave us a chance to lay low and cool down.

Wow, that was a scary experience, and the fact that the FRS were after us because they thought we stole the painting made everything a little more problematic. The FRS knew who I was, but the people who actually stole the painting off the yacht didn't. So from what I gather, the FRS want the painting back while the people who stole the painting are in the hunt for The Key to Miami, and I was stuck right in the centre of all this. The whole mission's difficulty had just been cranked up a notch.

CHAPTER 14

Showtime

Being in the mall on the top floor, Monty and I were anxious to leave. We shopped around for different clothes, and actually ended up going to a barber shop for a haircut, thinking that it would help disguise us from the FRS. The fashionable haircuts in Florida are presumably different to the preferences in England, with the haircuts we received coming out different to what I was expecting. Don't get me wrong, it wasn't the worst haircut in the world, but in hindsight I probably should have been a bit more specific on what I wanted rather than letting the barber decide. After a visit to the barbershop, we crossed over the road to a thrift store, buying some cheap sunglasses and a cap to help with our new appearance. Although I was confident that the disguise idea would work, I was still nervous that we'd be noticed. Regardless, we ploughed on through the day, staying positive at what was left of it.

Monty and I had managed to spend some time to cool down a bit, and were joined by Julia and Miguel. Getting some food at a nearby restaurant helped ease some nerves, as it was good to spend some time doing something completely unrelated to 'the mission'. In fact, I deliberately made an effort to divert any conversation away from the main mission, and it was easy, as it all quickly turned to the food. And the food....mm, it was absolutely delicious. I opted for a margarita pizza. It may sound boring, but trust me, at this restaurant a dull meal was impossible. In fact, the place was very fancy, with most of the menu being written in Spanish.

I didn't want to get something I didn't like, so with pizza being one of the few words on the menu I understood, it wasn't a hard choice for me. Everyone else went for something a little more...'exotic' to say the least. Miguel really pushed the boat out with his 'Ligatumsa'. Apparently this is a special Cuban dish consisting of Chicken and Vegetables. It didn't look like it though. I can't really give it a comparison to something in order to extrapolate what it was like, as I hadn't ever seen something edible that looked like it before. Chef's secret I suppose.

The time went by, and the moment soon came for Monty and I to head off for the game of the century (it was for me, as Westminster had the opportunity to officially be crowned the best football team on the planet). As Julia and Miguel didn't have tickets to the game, they both decided to go to a special screening event by the beachfront, with a huge screen and outdoor seating area. It was good weather for it to say the least. Our tickets were virtual ones on our phones, so we just needed to give the ticket officers a barcode for them to scan. The battery life was pretty low, and in the hope that it wouldn't run out, I kept mine switched off. I also sent a screenshot of it to Monty, as he would be able to scan mine on the machine using his phone just in case, so it looked like everything was going to be fine.

While we were on our way to the match, we were frantically discussing how we were going to get to the Phoenix Stadium in time, as we hadn't organised how we were actually going to get there. Apparently, the rules for the stadium stipulated that supporters who arrive more than 10 minutes after kick-off get turned away. Originally we had planned to get a taxi, but it was clear that this wasn't the best option, with the streets being jammed.

Julia and Miguel had no pressure to get to their destination on time – but we did! After they both went their separate way to us, Monty and I were inconclusive as to which mode of transport was the best one for us to take; we probably should have sorted it out beforehand. I then did a rapid internet search on transport links, and it was clear that catching a train up to the stadium was the best option. Ideally we would have used our bikes, but we didn't really fancy cycling across the other half of the city. In hindsight, this might have been the best method of transport for the situation that we were in.

When it came to booking train tickets, there weren't many free bookings left. However, because the nearest station was close to where we were (and to the stadium on the other end), it looked as if it would be a smooth ride. Thankfully, it was - there weren't any issues upon arriving at the stadium.

Being on the train with other Westminster fans was pretty cool. They seemed confident in the team's ability to pull off the victory. Even though we were in Miami, it felt like I was in the midst of a Westminster invasion with the amount of Blue Westminster shirts about. A blue wave had arrived at the shores of Miami; Westminster had arrived. As the stadium was about 15 miles away, we made quite a few stops along the way, picking up more and more football fans as each stop went by. I think it was clear that a lot of the fans didn't have tickets for the train, with several of them standing in the corridor of the train after all the seats had been taken.

Eventually, we arrived at the stadium. The station where we got off was literally next-door to it, making everything incredibly convenient. Soaking up the electric atmosphere, Monty and I went to get some souvenirs. For this match, both teams were going to be wearing a limited-edition shirt for the occasion, and of course, I just had to get one to remember the event by. Monty got a Phoenix shirt, while I was about to get the Westminster one that was designed with the famous blue colour that the club were renowned for wearing. However, I then remembered about the signed football shirt from Jenkins. From the messages I received from him, he told me that one would be waiting for me in the merchandise store, inside the stadium. Sure enough, one was there waiting for me. I was thrilled and put it on straight away upon receiving it.

After we had got our shirts, we both eventually arrived at our seats just as the two teams walked out onto the pitch. I then bit into a scrumptious beef burger again, soaking up more of the atmosphere. Life. Was. Good. After attending the English Cup Final earlier in May, I didn't think that any other football experience would top it, but trust me, this did. The national anthems for the UK and the USA were sung for both teams. After the pre-match team photographs had been taken, and once the teams were in position, the referee blew his whistle for the match to get underway.

Well, the pre-match excitement was as good as it got for me over the next hour or so, with some pretty drab football being put on show. It looked like Miami had decided to park the bus from the get go, while Westminster were playing so casually, passing the ball around the defence, it looked as if they were playing in an exhibition. I think that because they were given so much time on the ball by Miami, they stopped playing with the same intensity that they would usually play with in a league game back in England. Arguably, some of the teams in Europe were harder to play against. But still, on their day, Miami are one of the best teams out there.

Looking at the half-time statistics didn't surprise me at all – there had only been one shot in the entire match by this point, and that was from Charlie Trundle blazing a 30-yard free-kick over the bar. I guessed that the only positive from the first-half was that things could only get better (well, I was hoping that, anyway).

This was exactly the case. Immediately once the second half commenced, the whole complexion of the game changed – it was as if I was watching a completely different match. There was more energy, passion and risks being taken. Crunching tackles were flying in from all over the park, adding to the tension that was growing as each attack developed. However, with there still not being many clear-cut-chances, and the tension growing and growing inside the stadium, things suddenly got out of hand and boiled over after a Miami midfielder, Sammy Barnes, flew in with a wild, two-footed challenge on Charlie Trundle, just as Trundle was about to shoot. Trundle managed to get the shot away, and it was a ferocious one indeed, rattling the crossbar before going out of play for a goal kick.

However, the damage to Trundle's ankle was the main talking point from this part of the match. At the time he looked to be in considerable pain, and I was sure that Barnes was going to get sent off for the challenge. The Westminster players were clearly upset as well. Several players were booked for their role in the small brawl that emerged in the immediate aftermath of the poorly-timed challenge, and shockingly, Barnes only got a yellow card for the tackle (even though Trundle had to be substituted with a serious-looking injury).

Micky Ryan came on as a substitute to replace Trundle. Watching the game, I was hoping that he could make some sort of impact. Since he got injured back in 2012, he hadn't really had the impact that was expected from him (although, he had shown glimpses of his potential). Once replays of the foul were played back on the big screen, gasps of anger and surprise could be heard ringing out from around the stadium replicating the sound effects of an echo chamber, as each angle of the tackle was replayed several times. The camera then zoomed in onto the referee like a spotlight of shame, once the play had commenced again, and judging from his expressions, I think he knew that he had messed up by not showing a red card to Barnes.

Surprisingly, the overall temperament of the game slowed down following on from this. Westminster still continued to dominate the match; however, against the run of play, Jackson Tyler managed to win the ball in the centre of the pitch by tackling Roger Jenkins. Tyler then ran with the ball, weaving in and out of the oncoming Westminster players as if they were stationary practice cones. Being in an uncomfortable position to shoot, he held the ball up before picking out a pass to Sammy Barnes who was on the edge of the box. Shooting first time, Barnes produced a rasping shot that flew into the top corner of the goal. 1-0 to Miami Phoenix!

It was clear the Barnes shouldn't have been on the pitch, and seeing him score a goal that could potentially end the chances of Westminster winning the biggest prize in football left a sour taste in my mouth. To make everything worse, Barnes even had the cheek to overtly celebrate in front of the Westminster fans who were sitting behind the same goal that the ball flew into. Although this was all incredibly frustrating, I was confident that Westminster would find a goal from somewhere with the time remaining in the match.

The goal injected a sense of urgency into the Westminster team, as within sixty seconds of the restart, Roger Jenkins popped up in the centre of the box and connected with a fine cross from the right wing, causing the ball to fly past the goalkeeper, ripping the back of the net. 1-1, and game on! The game only got better from here as with the next attack, Jenkins scored again! After doing literally nothing all game, Jenkins had suddenly scored two goals in the most important match in Westminster's history, in two minutes! 1-2. This goal was a typical striker's finisher. Immediately winning the ball off a Miami player after the restart, Micky Ryan threaded through a beautiful pass to Jenkins, splitting the defence in half like an experienced chef slicing a cake for a hungry customer in a café. It was a spectacular pass! Jenkins then found himself 1-on-1 with the goalkeeper, before stroking the ball past him and into the back of the net. It was amazing to watch. That Barnes goal had really woken the Westminster players up. In a way it was probably a blessing in disguise that Westminster conceded that Barnes goal, as the game could otherwise have fizzled out into a 0-0 draw. You just never know what would have happened, I suppose.

The score stayed at 1-2 for some time after the quick-fire double from Jenkins. Because Miami had to move more players forward in search of an equaliser, it left a lot more space for Westminster to counterattack. Jenkins missed a great chance to secure the game, missing an easy header with the goal gaping from a counterattack, with only ten minutes remaining. It would've completed a remarkable hat-trick for him as well.

In the last minute of the match, the referee awarded a free kick to Miami Phoenix on the edge of the box for a foul on Buck Brown, Butch's uncle. Brown had been troubling the Westminster defence all game, and had been fouled by the Westminster right-back, John McGregor. This looked like it would be the last attack of the game, and judging from the angle of the kick in relation to the goal, the obvious option for Miami would be to cross the ball in, but in football (and with the skill that Buck Brown possessed) you just never know for certain what is about to happen!

Buck Brown looked like he was ready to step up and take the free-kick, but out of the corner of his eye I think he noticed that his own goalkeeper was making his way into the box. As the Miami goalkeeper had come up for the attack, it looked as if there was a lot of potential for some last-minute drama. The Miami goalkeeper was clearly trying to be a nuisance for the Westminster defenders. With everyone ready to attack or defend the ball, Buck Brown finally took the free-kick.

What happened next surprised us all. Rather than cross the ball in, Brown tricked most of the players (and me) by blasting the ball directly towards the goal with a fair amount of power behind the shot. The ball hit the inside of the post, and literally rolled across the face of the open goal. The ball then fell to Sammy Barnes who somehow completely missed the ball with his attempt. One of the Westminster defenders, Alex Foster, then got to the ball and hoofed it clear up the pitch. Roger Jenkins, who was the only player on the half-way line, was free to collect the ball – he was all alone. Instead of controlling the ball, Jenkins volleyed the ball first time towards the goal. Without bouncing, the ball flew through the Miami air at high speed and hit the back of the net. What a goal to complete a hat-trick for Roger Jenkins! It was the final kick of the game, and one worthy of sealing an ICC Final match. Westminster Warriors had done it. They were the champions of the world!

CHAPTER 15

Getting Late

Wow, what a game that was! Monty and I decided to stay after the match to witness the winner's ceremony. It was a pretty cool experience to see Westminster win the biggest club competition in the world. What a day. Everything soon calmed down, which was perhaps because the crowd came to the realisation of having to navigate their way through the Miami traffic outside the Phoenix Stadium. That included Monty and I – we needed to find a way back to the house. Upon leaving the stadium, I began to wonder about Millie and how she was in relation to finding the key. In the end she decided to go out alone after hanging out with Butch and his team a little bit longer than Monty and I had. She was aware of the FRS being in the city (thanks to some messages I had sent her earlier), so if she actually made it to the

Miami Tower unnoticed, it would be some sort of progress.

Upon leaving the stadium, I received some good news, with a pleasant notification bringing a smile to my face. Not only had Millie managed to sneak into the tower, but she had also found a way up to the cupola of the building. There, she had actually found the place where the historic painting was presumably from. After a lot of perseverance and patience, she found a loose brick with an 'X' etched onto it. The 'X' was really small, with it only being after the second time of looking that she spotted it. As I wasn't there at the time, all the information that I knew was from the messages I had received from her. After using some special gadgets that she bought with her to loosen the brick, what she saw next was extraordinary – inside the brick she saw it. It was The Key to Miami! After taking a load of pictures, she carefully picked up the shiny, gold key with some latex gloves, revealing some text etched into the underside of the brick. It read: *The Key to Miami – 1929, E.G.* Obviously, it was imprinted with the initials for Enrico Gonzalez – It was definitely the key! The image was the last message of a flurry of messages that I had received from Millie. I'm guessing that she had to be very careful with her next steps.

Noticing that she hadn't messaged for a while, I texted her to see where she was headed. I presumed that it was back at Monty's house, but it could also be at the apartment Butch had been staying at, close to the race circuit. Even though Butch had just taken part in a fast-paced race, it wouldn't surprise me if she went to visit him, as with Butch this was sort of a safe haven with the amount of security that was in place for the teams that participated in the Florida Race Series.

I also wondered whether she was still at the tower, looking for the door that the key unlocked. The fact that she hadn't messaged in a while did make me slightly curious. After messaging Butch, who then replied that he hadn't heard from her since the early afternoon, I presumed that her phone had run out of battery. Yes, in the back of my mind there was that squeaky recurring thought that she had run into trouble, but I trusted that she would be okay. As she had already visited and researched the Miami Tower, I was confident that she would be fine and prepared for any sticky situation that may occur.

We thought about going back to the house, but as we were in Miami, and with the city lights shining brighter than ever, Monty said that this would be a good opportunity to go down to the beach and chill. I still hadn't been down to the beach at this point, and so going over there to relax seemed like a cool thing to do (while it was also a good way for me to celebrate the Westminster triumph – perhaps not so much for Monty though).

Having watched the game on the big screen at the 'fan view' area near South Beach, Julia and Miguel were also nearby in a convenient place to join us. Before meeting them, Monty and I went to get a few things on the way. We both bought a drink, and in looking for a football to play with on the beachfront, Monty spotted some cheap boxing gloves and gave me a cheeky look as if to say 'go on'. Monty had already made it known that he could throw a punch, as he sometimes went along to the Miami Amateur Boxing Academy to get coached by the professional who was there: Hugo Yaakov. At first, I was thinking 'no-way', but since we weren't going to be fighting for real, and that it was just going to be for fun, I gave in and agreed to have a go. We bought a pair of gloves each.

On the way over to South Beach, we went past hundreds of football fans. The football fan area however, had pretty much been deserted. There were only a few Westminster fans there, as well as some litter pickers cleaning up the huge amount of mess that had been left behind.

Arriving at the beach, I breathed in the fresh night breeze that had descended onto the waters of Miami. The climate was phenomenal. I was there, with my eyes closed, outstretching my arms, enjoying the moment. However, after a small friendly punch from Monty, it dawned on me that he was actually serious about doing a bit of boxing. I was pretty nervous about this (although I tried not to show it), and once it was evident to Monty that I didn't even know how to throw a proper 'boxing-style' punch, the proposed sparring session turned into a coaching lesson.

From teaching me about foot position and how to 'jab', as well as the importance of always having my guard up, it was evident that Monty had learnt a lot from Yaakov's coaching. As we didn't have any punching pads, Monty held up his gloves for me to direct my punches, helping me improve my power and accuracy. Apparently, the precision of my punches was pretty good for a first-timer. This was actually quite encouraging considering that he'd trained hard with other guys my age who had had previous boxing experience. After throwing a few more practice punches, Monty gave me a nugget of wisdom for how to improve the power behind my jabs. From his sessions with Yaakov, Monty demonstrated that most of the power doesn't come from the fists or the arms, but from the legs and hips. By twisting my hips in the correct fashion, he said that I would be able to generate more power when punching. After altering my hip movement, the change in the power was immediately noticeable. Monty then taught me a few more combinations. The time flew by, and all of a sudden we had been training for about half-an-hour.

I was focusing on the boxing skills so much, that I didn't even notice Miguel and Julia come over until I had finished the last few pad combinations that Monty had instructed me to do. I was quite tired at this point and needed a rest, making it quite convenient that Miguel and Julia had come over when they did. One of their friends, Kiera, had also come over.

Miguel arriving gave me a chance to tell him about the finding of the key. I showed him the video and his reaction was a pleasant one to say the least. He went on to emphasise how much it all meant to him and his family. It was pretty cool that I was actually interacting with a relative of Gonzalez himself. With the key found, we only needed to find the door that the key unlocked (and that was, if Millie hadn't already found it), leading us to the paintings.

It was beginning to get late. We had a good time down at the beach, but speaking of Millie, my curiosity grew in relation to where she was. So, the

156

five of us together went back to the centre of Brickell before Monty and I went our separate way back to the house. Yet, there was something noticeable that caught my attention and unnerved me a bit. I didn't tell anyone what it was, but it made me slightly anxious about Millie's possible situation.

You see, when we passed by a load of parked boats on the way to Brickell, I immediately recognised the yacht I stumbled onto when I was in France. While out on Brian's boat, I thought I saw the same boat, but noticing the letters 'FRS' on the side of the boat I was 99.9% sure that it was the same yacht as the one that I went on in France. Knowing how dangerous the tenants of the boat could be, I kind of feared for my safety in case they were nearby. Not only did they want to retrieve the painting, but I reckon that they also knew of the key. As Vernon and I were the ones who were chased off the boat, it wouldn't surprise me if I had a target on my back. It was mighty likely that they thought Vernon and I were responsible for the painting's disappearance, when in actuality it was two other guys (who were the men actually hunting for the key).

However, they may also be out to steal the painting back from the two men who mysteriously entered the boat in France. If Millie encountered the two henchmen, or anyone from the FRS at the Miami

Tower, this could be why she wasn't answering her phone. I checked my messages again, to see if I had had any new messages from Millie. Still no reply.

I then took a picture of the boat I had suspicions about, and after comparing this image with the picture of the boat in France, I was able to tell that they were definitely the same. I messaged Butch the pictures and told him about my suspicions, just to keep him in the loop.

Naturally, I walked back to the house at a faster pace than usual, and because of the frantic speed, I felt as if I needed to tell Monty about the boat and how things had potentially become quite serious. After explaining the situation to him, he was on board with where I was at, and went with me to see if Millie had arrived back at the house. It wasn't long before we arrived ourselves. Members of Monty's family were there, but after asking if Millie was back, and looking around the house for her, it was evident that Millie wasn't anywhere to be seen. We had to think positively, as there was a good chance that she was okay, in a safe place. Yet the fact she still wasn't answering her phone, and with that boat moored in Miami, I was still a bit concerned. Even though Butch had to be up early the next day to do some analysis evaluation on his car performance with the senior principle of his race team, he messaged me to say that he would look around the Miami Tower (and the area nearby) to see if he could find Millie before he went to sleep. Because he had raced so well, he said there would also be further meetings about him doing more races (even if one of the reserve drivers were to be available again). Butch helping was incredibly helpful, considering that he was probably exhausted from the race and his media obligations. The guy's a legend.

I also considered whether to go out into the late night to search for Millie, but as Butch had already said he would be going out to look with a friend of his, I thought that I'd be better off getting a good night's sleep. I didn't want to make things worse and get lost myself, as this would be really stupid if Millie was totally fine. Monty concurred having already decided to stay. Yet I had a gut-feeling that I should go out and look for her regardless. I tried to sleep everything off, but after tossing and turning in bed for about an hour or so I made up my mind. That was it. I decided to go out and look for Millie. I messaged Butch to let him know I was going. I told Monty, who was still awake, what I intended to do. Not wanting to miss out on anything, he chose to come as well. We both quietly snuck out of the house, embracing the open Miami night breeze. As the old Chinese proverb goes: a one thousand mile journey begins with a single step, and although I wouldn't be going that far, I took a step in the right direction, hoping that I would finally be able to put my mind to rest. Joining me in the quest, Monty came with me, not knowing what was to come next. Miami called, and I was there to pick up.

CHAPTER 16

The Miami Tower

It was dark (and late). I'm glad that Monty came along, as I've heard that Miami can be a dangerous place at night if you don't know what you're doing. I knew where I was going - I just wasn't sure how safe each particular area of Miami was. Monty did though, and he was able to lead the way to the Miami Tower for us both. The nightlife in Miami was notorious for being quite 'vibrant' to say the least. Even in the early hours of the morning there were still a lot of people hanging around. We'd organised a rendezvous point for meeting up with Butch and his pal, Bruce. It wasn't the Miami Tower itself, but it was pretty close in a relatively safe place.

We soon found Butch and Bruce and met up with them. The four of us were there in the middle of

Miami at night, looking to enter into the historic tower in our hopes of finding Millie (or look for possible traces that may provide an indicator for where she was). We came to the conclusion that we needed to come up with a plan away from the tower, as we didn't want to be seen hanging around outside it, attracting any sort of suspicion. We soon came up with a plan. Here, we aimed to climb up onto a lower ledge, and then gradually climb up from there.

The whole thing wasn't well thought out with the limited time that we gave ourselves, while it was also nonchalantly dangerous. It seemed too far-fetched for my liking, and being really tired, I wasn't exactly confident. We came up to the tower just to scout out the area, and our decision was made for us when we saw some police cars surrounding the tower with sirens. It seemed clear that they were aware of a something going on in association with the tower, yet there didn't seem to be anyone near or inside it (apart from us). If anyone was inside, they had done a pretty good job at hiding it. Hanging around from a distance, it didn't look like we were going to get anywhere. In fact, by loitering near the area, our situation would probably spiral downward as the police may approach us on suspicion of us being culprits who had broken in. The risk vs reward outcome didn't weigh up in our favour considering the circumstances that we found ourselves in. Obviously, we wanted to find Millie, yet it seemed like we had run out of reasonable options to choose from after taking everything into account.

From this point, and as hard as it was, the best option was to go again the next day at a time when we would all be refreshed, albeit Bruce and Butch who would probably be busy discussing the possibility of further races. Monty and I then went back to the house while Bruce and Butch went to their apartments. Back at the house, I went to sleep, and literally had no idea what the next day would bring.

CHAPTER 17

Room 477

I slept in again. And man, it was pretty late. The sun was shining brighter than the previous day and it felt like a proper good Monday. I had woken up in a whirlwind-like state and was a bit confused at what had actually happened. I felt like I needed to be concerned or worried about something, yet I wasn't sure what it was. Monty was already up, being useful, assisting in fixing a door hinge. The one in the corridor had come a bit loose and so he was holding it still for someone to tighten up the screws, making it a lot more secure than previously. By the time I was out of bed, I had been asked to help paint the garden fences. I was actually happy to do this, and thankfully I was given half an hour or so to make my breakfast and get some appropriate clothes on before getting to work.

My usual option for breakfast in England is a generous bowl of Choco Munch-Munch cereal (the Cinnamon Munch-Munch cereal that has been introduced by Gordy's (the brand that makes Munch-Munch cereals) is incredibly tasty, but I don't think that this new variety tops the formula for the chocolate version), but unfortunately I have yet to find a store that sells it in Florida. With my favourite choice of cereal out of the window, I settled for oatmeal, sprinkled with cinnamon (yes, I do like cinnamon) and dashed with drizzles of honey. In all honesty, I probably should have known that we didn't have any Choco Munch-Munch, but I guess that I just felt a bit dazed from the late night out. Tucking into the delicious oatmeal, I remembered the reason behind my late night in the middle of Miami: Millie had been missing. I checked my phone to see if there were any messages from her. Still nothing. I needed to look for her, but I had a fence to paint that I felt obliged to do. Reading my messages, I learnt that there were other people out looking for Millie, while Monty said he planned to go out with Julia, Miguel, and Kiera to look around for where she may be.

Wanting to get the job done and dusted, I quickly got on with the painting while thinking about my next steps for the day. Painting is definitely something I'd like to do more of in the future, with it

165

proving to be quite therapeutic. It always feels good when you can look back at a job that you've done and think to yourself 'I did that'. The weather had been decent as well with the setting proving to be a seemingly perfect fit for painting a backyard fence. I had some nice music on that suited the conditions, and even though I was working relatively hard, the whole situation was actually kind of luxurious. This was especially the case when someone kindly brought out for me a cup of iced coffee, along with a couple of biscuits. I consumed both within five minutes of receiving them. Refreshing and delicious! While at first it took a while for me to get to grips with using the brush to its full effectiveness, I soon found a routine where I was able to glide through each panel at a consistent and speedy pace. Before I knew it, I had managed to complete the job.

Ping. I received a message. In the anticipation and excitement, I accidently knocked the paint can that I was using over, narrowly missing my phone that was on the side by the spare paintbrush. I was hoping that this message would be from Millie, or even news about her and...it was! It was from Millie herself, but from what I read, her situation didn't look too good. The message wasn't actually from Millie's personal phone, and the only reason that I knew it was her was because in the message it said 'from Millie' (I guess

166

that is kind of obvious, but I thought that I'd say, to be clear). The message was very brief, indicating that she didn't have much time to compose it. With other people after the key also, to me it seemed likely that she had found herself in the middle of a greater search for the key.

Importantly, Millie had also shared an address as part of the message. I quickly forwarded this to Butch and Monty, while also messaging other people the news. I looked up the address on the map app on my phone, and from the images it looked like the address belonged to a really nice, plush apartment block near the beach. Putting the pieces that I had together, it was likely that she had been trapped in this apartment at the time of the text, while the guys who captured her had probably stolen the key from her (unless she had hidden it somewhere before she was inadvertently caught in the tower).

I thought about going to the address straight away, yet I was also aware of the need to be careful and calculated in regards to my approach, just in case this whole thing was a trap: we needed a plan. This plan also had to be without Butch, due to his racing duties associated with the team. Although, he said that he was still free in the evening after 6 p.m., which was somewhat helpful.

The city had calmed slightly since the weekend, but it was still hectic, with some streets closed due to the clear up of the race circuit. Regardless of how the city was, I knew it was highly probable that Millie had been captured by a group of criminals at this moment in time. What made the situation scary was that the FRS, or some other group, were probably lurking around Miami (or in the Miami Tower itself) with the key, looking for the hidden collection of goodies left by Gonzalez for his family (which Miguel was part of). Yes, I wanted to go to the apartment and help Millie escape, but I needed to do it with finesse and be very calculated in my approach, just in case the whole thing was a trap (I mean, they could have been the ones who sent out the text message to me).

So, I dropped everything that I was doing, before calling Monty, who also went out with me to scout out the area around the apartment where Millie was said to be, properly formulating a plan for how we would 'strike'. Miami was a big city, and not only would walking around take a long time, but it would also be quite tiring. So, using the bikes that we had collected from where we last left them, we sped up towards the address that was on the message I received from Millie.

The address was literally right on the beachfront in a tall block of flats, and by the looks of things, the room in the address (room 477) was smack-bang on the top floor. If Millie was in there, it would be tricky for her to escape out of the window. Next we sneaked into the main building and had a look around. To stop us making too much noise, I asked Monty to position himself at the end of the corridor, next to the lift, in order to stand on the look-out whilst I slowly tiptoed up to the room.

Then suddenly, I heard a turning of the door handle – it was about to open. There wasn't really anyway for me to take cover, but thankfully I was able to dive behind the corner of the corridor just in time. This didn't help much though, as the person who came out of the room headed straight for the lift. Monty seemed to be on the same wavelength as me and had already activated the lift to go down. Although, I asked myself; should we take the stairs or wait for the lift?

Thinking on our toes, I decided to take the stairs while Monty took the lift. Unfortunately, the person I was trying to stay clear of chose to take the stairs down too. Noticing this, I didn't run, as I didn't want to create too much noise, and so I quickly left the stairwell by entering the next corridor on the floor below, hoping that I didn't get followed. I didn't, phew.

I messaged Monty to let him know where I was, and after the close call, we were able to get some respite and plan our way forward again. If Millie was in the apartment, we presumed that there would only be one other person. There were two who took the painting off the yacht. If it wasn't an FRS apartment, perhaps the guy inside was the mastermind behind stealing the painting off the yacht.

Originally, we had decided to help save Millie when it was dark, with it being easier to sneak around stealthily. Yet, with one of the guys gone from the apartment, it seemed like a good opportunity to devise a plan on the spot. We wanted to adapt to a change in circumstances – it seemed like the best option

As I had been recognised by the FRS, our plan was for Monty to execute a 'knock and run' exercise. The person holding up the fort would then hopefully hear Monty say that he's going to report everyone in the apartment to the police, to goad the person into start chasing after him, giving me a free run at searching the premises. So, this time we reversed the rolls. I waited on the floor on the other side of the corridor. It was important that I went in quickly when the door was open and that the bandit inside followed Monty blindly, without taking any of his surroundings into account. It was nearly showtime, and ready for our plan to commence.

So, sneaking onto the other side of the corridor, I waited for Monty to knock and run. Creeping up to room 477 of *Miami Heights*, it was fair to say that Monty looked pretty nervous. Incredibly nervous, actually. He had a game plan of escaping through the fire exit, and mixing in with everyone on the extremely busy beach. It was risky, but with the sun blazing and the beach crowded, it would be hard to chase someone on it as well. Monty also knew Miami like the back of his hand. If anyone could evade a potentially highly dangerous member of a criminal organisation, I reckon that Monty had the skills and know-how to do this.

Finally, Monty came up to the door of room 477, and gave it a loud double-knock. He didn't run straight away, as he needed to make sure that the door opened. After about two seconds, no one had come to the door, making us wonder whether anyone was actually in. I signalled to Monty that he should have a go, one more time. So, Monty went up again and gave it anther knock. This time, Monty accidently knocked someone in the face, as the person in the room opened the door, just as Monty knocked. Let's just say that the man at the door didn't look too pleased that he had just basically been thumped in the face – I probably wouldn't be too pleased either.

Immediately, Monty said he would call the police and then legged it. The man didn't look too pleased again and ran straight after Monty. Interestingly, the man was wearing uniform for staff members who work at the Miami Tower (either he worked there, or he was disguising himself as one). Momentarily, the door was left wide open before it was about to close. Just in the nick of time, I managed to make my way to the door like a ninja and put my foot in the door, just before it closed. Phew! Without much time to lose (for various reasons to be honest with you) I carefully finessed my way into the main part of the apartment. Before I got relatively comfortable with the surroundings and searched for Millie and the key, I looked around the apartment to see if anyone else was there. But wow, the apartment was huge. It had about four different bedrooms, a huge kitchen, dining room, as well as a large lounge area. On the table in one of the rooms, I noticed what looked like a lot of interesting Intel related to Gonzalez's treasure. I wanted to explore this room further, but finding Millie was still the priority.

Then, entering one of the bathrooms, I came across someone handcuffed to the bathtub. It was Millie! From where she was, she did well to send a text, but she also looked in a rough state. She had a lot to tell me, even mentioning to me that the key had been taken from her. Monty was presumably doing a fantastic job in giving us a free-run, but we knew the possibility of the henchman being back at any second was high.

With Millie handcuffed, it was easier said than done to free her. Our search for keys went from one to two. What was it about keys that make them so relevant to pretty much everything I had done in recent times? My trip to *Kurt's Keys* seemed like such a long time ago, yet that was only about three months or so prior to finding myself in no. 477 of *Miami Heights*. Life moves fast.

Fortunately, I managed to find the key for the handcuffs within 30 seconds. It was literally in the first place that I looked, underneath one of the plant pots! Easy! Millie was finally able to feel a glimpse of freedom, and so after going into the table room, I took as many pictures of the group's findings and hurriedly continued my search for the key (if it was even in the apartment).

It was really scary being in this room. It was very dark and dingy with papers, files and photographs spread out and stuck all over the table and wall. It was as if there was an enemy operation to take down the government taking place before our eyes. There were even maps of where they looked to find The Key to Miami first (before going to the Miami Tower). By the looks of things, they had arrived in Miami shortly after stealing the painting off the boat in France. These were the guys who the FRS should be upset with – not Vernon and I.

And that's when I saw it, the painting! As soon as I saw it, memories from my little trip on the yacht in Boulogne headed back to me. It felt like a month had gone by since it happened, yet it was only about a week or so. While I was gazing at the painting reminiscing the previous fortnight's events, Millie pointed to a vault that looked interesting to say the least. After many attempts, we weren't able to open it, and it looked like we didn't have a chance, since it needed a fingerprint for it to be opened.

We were adamant that this is where the key was, but after wandering around, looking for any sort of method to find and use a fingerprint that belonged to a henchman from around the house, I came across something sitting on the tea table by the TV, in the main room. It was this gold, glaring shiny key. It was actually pretty big as well. Part of me was sure that this was The Key to Miami, but then again, I was confident that criminals or this calibre wouldn't just leave a key of this value out in the open. However, after further inspection and actually noticing some writing on the key that Millie spotted was the same as the writing that was on the key in some of the photos that Millie had sent me, I had no doubt. This was the key. I finally had it in my hand. It was in my possession. I had found The Key to Miami! The person who went after Monty must have been observing the key before getting up to answer the door.

CHAPTER 18

Bittersweet

I went to alert Millie of my findings, and it was great to see that she was as excited as I was in regards to finding the key. We had everything that we came for. Next, we just needed to get out, but also make sure that Monty was okay. Just as I was calling Monty, I heard heavy footsteps, and they sounded like they were coming straight for room 477! I had to turn my phone off so that it didn't make any noise, putting my call with Monty on hold. With there only being one door that entered into the apartment, our best bet was to hide and wait for a chance to go through the main door for our escape. As the key was no longer on the table, it would be likely that the guy knew he had been duped, but whether he knew we were in the apartment is another matter. Millie hid behind one of the doors that opened up, while I hid behind the sofa (which was definitely a risky move). In came the man who had chased after Monty. As Monty wasn't there with him, I guessed that he had managed to make a getaway. My phone was completely out of juice, and so I had no way of knowing, but I still had confidence in Monty and was sure that he had made it home safely.

My plan was to leave as soon as possible, I wasn't able to communicate this with Millie, as she was in a different room, but once Derek (I noticed he was wearing a name tag that seemed to be part of his uniform) dashed into what seemed to be the operation control room (after he had screamed at the fact that the key was missing) I made a run for it. Unfortunately, I tripped over after climbing over the sofa, hitting my knee on the tea table, creating a loud thud. From the moment I tripped, I knew I was in trouble. Derek must have heard this as he came rushing into the room that I was in, giving me a glaring look as I opened up the door. I'd never seen someone look that angry in my life (I suppose the Gonzalez treasure was probably worth a lot of dosh). This was a very dangerous situation that I had landed myself in, but at least it gave Millie a free run to leave.

The adrenaline was pumping like I'd never known before, and my survival instincts had properly kicked in. It was similar to the time that I outran

Connor, but in this situation it was a lot more intense. However, the threat of Connor was like that of a harmless rabbit compared to Derek, and I must say that Monty did very well if he managed to evade Derek. This was like having a hungry lion galloping after its prey (this is just going by what it's like in some documentaries I've watched as I've never actually been chased by a lion before). I was actually chased by a bull one time, but that's a whole different story.

So I scurried down the corridor, and headed for the open elevator. I was just hoping that it wouldn't close on me. Unfortunately though, it did, and in a split second I had to immediately change my course of action. It felt disastrous at the time, but I was just thankful that I had the stairs available to my right hand side.

Rushing down the stairs, Derek had nearly caught up with me, but every time he was within a metre of me, I found an extra amount of energy from somewhere and accelerated further with an additional burst of speed. I hoped I wouldn't bump into any of Derek's entourage.

He obviously wasn't the fittest person out there, with his energy levels clearly waning as I neared the ground floor. I was about to go out of the main entrance, but remembered the plan: use the back door to get out. This is where the bikes were parked up. It then dawned on me that I would need to unlock the bike cable in good time without Derek coming after me. I reckoned that I had about 10 seconds before he caught up with me. Rushing out of the building, I reached into my pocket to get the cable key ready. I managed to swiftly unlock the bike in one sweeping motion. I fastened my helmet (that I was surprised no one had stolen, and I was ready to roll! Derek then came out, and noticing that I was about to leave, gave one big dive after me. He completely missed though, and probably hurt himself from diving on the slab of concrete. I headed for the centre of Brickell, hoping that I would be able to go down some alleys to shake Derek off. With Derek chasing after me, it seemed very likely that Millie had managed to escape, however the whereabouts of her and Monty weren't explicitly known to me. Still not knowing my way around Miami, Brickell seemed to be the best destination point, as I was somewhat comfortable going there having visiting the area multiple times with my friends.

Feeling slightly paranoid in regards to Derek's exact location, I headed over the bridge and thought I had made it to the city centre safety. However, a motorbike came soaring towards me from behind, looking like it was headed straight for me. It was easy to recognise who the rider was, as he wasn't even wearing a helmet: it was Derek! Obviously, from being on the old bike that I was on, there would be little chance of me outpacing him. Yet, this wasn't like most bikes. The bike it was most similar to is probably the now destroyed Verntron, as I secretly had the bike taken to a special bikes mod shop to get a few modifications after Butch's race, with one of these being a turbo boost setting. This was nowhere near as powerful as the Verntron, but putting some of my knowledge that I had learned from Vernon, I was able to direct the bike engineers towards the modification I wanted.

The bike modification definitely gave me an extra edge. As I didn't think that the bike was designed to go 30mph - I was actually quite worried about the wheels coming off. Nevertheless, the Verntron-inspired modification was potentially life-saving, helping me to avoid the clutches of Derek. I was sure that the some of the other members of Derek's gang would be onto me soon (or out looking for Millie or Monty) as the key was instrumental to finding the Gonzalez treasure. I just hoped that no one knew about Miguel, Julia, or Butch's involvement, as the last thing that I wanted was for the livelihoods of other people to be at risk because of me!

I had no idea where everyone else was, but from making a turn into an alley in the city centre, it seemed that everyone from Derek's group was on me (I also needed to be aware of the FRS too), as Derek had clearly called for back-up. It was now three on one. I knew that I wouldn't be able to outpace three guys who were on motorbikes forever. I was tempted to give up and throw in the towel, as I didn't want to risk injuring myself: any human life is more valuable than any amount of treasure. Perhaps the right thing to do would be to give them the key and cut my losses. At least this way they would all stop coming after me.

It was looking like I was going to do this, as we headed towards the waters. I had to swerve to my right at the last second to stop myself from riding straight into the railings, and into the sea. I was pretty sure that part of my back tyre scraped the railings after I turned. I then found myself riding down the pavement by the waterfront, approaching all of the moored boats. People were constantly jumping out the way of me on my bike, and the trailing motorbikes, not wanting to get injured. I felt awful at the time. Up ahead I then noticed a familiar sighting. It was Brian's boat! Not having enough space to properly stop, I jumped off the bike as I approached the boat, rolling several times in the process. The bike flew into the sea, hitting a boat on the way in, before sinking to the bottom of the sea. Glug.

Still with Derek's entourage chasing me, I got up and freed the boat, before jumping into it. I hoped that Brian would understand my decision. I knew where everything in Brian's hut was kept, so before Derek and co arrived, I already had the boat on its way out. Honestly it was a shame about the bike. Looking back, I was curious whether Derek would jump into the water and swim after me, or instead use one of the other boats. I was already out in front, so the only way they would get me was if they found another boat. I was also hoping that I didn't bump into the FRS while out at sea, as that would probably be more than I could handle.

The light was beginning to dim, and my body was crying out for rest, yet I knew of the dangers of stopping in the middle of the sea. I needed to find a safe and convenient place to moor the boat, although I didn't know where. I checked my pockets to see if I still had The Key to Miami in my possession. I did. But I did suffer a significant loss – my phone was gone! That was a bit of a disaster, but nonetheless, I was still alive.

So, there I was on my own on Brian's boat, not knowing where to go or who to contact. Miami wasn't a safe place for me. It proposed danger. I sailed into the sunset thinking of answers. Yes, I had The Key to Miami in my possession, but I had two different groups of dangerous people after me. I was safe in the boat, but at the same time I wasn't. Where should I go from here?